BBC
DOCTOR WHO

Silhouette

BBC
DOCTOR WHO

Silhouette

Justin Richards

B\D\W\Y
Broadway Books
New York

Library of Congress Cataloging-in-Publication Data is available upon request

ISBN 978-0-8041-4088-1
eBook ISBN 978-0-8041-4089-8

Printed in the United States of America

Editorial director: Albert DePetrillo
Series consultant: Justin Richards
Project editor: Steve Tribe
Cover design: Lee Binding © Woodlands Books Ltd 2014
Production: Alex Goddard

10 9 8 7 6 5 4 3 2 1

First U.S. Edition

For Alison,
as ever

Prologue

Marlowe Hapworth spent the majority of his last afternoon at the Frost Fair. There was a bite in the January air and he could feel the tingle of frost forming at the edges of his moustache. The snow crunched pleasantly beneath his feet. He laughed as a snowball whistled past his ear, waving encouragement to the urchin who had hurled it at a friend.

He stood for a moment on the Embankment, watching the skaters on the frozen river describing curved shapes on the ice before the Palace of Westminster. He blew out a stream of misty breath, letting it hang in the air as he listened to the laughter and reflected on the joys of being young. How pleasant to be carefree, at least for a while. An afternoon away from his studies, and then back to work in the morning, Hapworth decided.

Further along the river, he found the Frost Fair. It sprawled along the bank of the Thames and out onto the ice. Tents and stalls, sideshows and attractions.

Hapworth hurled wooden balls at coconuts that he suspected were fixed to their poles. Not that he minded in the least. He watched a man on stilts, sure-footed in the snow, juggling first with skittles and then with burning torches. He ate chestnuts so hot they scalded the roof of his mouth.

And at the end of a line of stalls selling everything from carved wooden animals to muffins, from brittle toffee to lace kerchiefs, he found a sign pointing him to the Carnival of Curiosities. Set slightly apart from the rest of the Frost Fair, the 'Carnival' seemed to be a combination of circus, fair, and exhibition. Hapworth paid a penny for admission to the lad at the gate, and then wandered fascinated through the carnival.

A strongman, stripped to the waist, his upper body covered in tattoos juggled with medicine balls laughing all the while. A gypsy woman sat at a table, peering into a crystal ball. Various tents advertised their contents as 'The Amazing Bearded Woman', 'A Genuine Wolf Boy', 'Never-Creatures – animals not of Nature' and other intriguing and enticing attractions. He paid more pennies to laugh and cringe and marvel at them all.

Most fascinating was the Shadowplay. From his time in India and the Far East, Hapworth had an appreciation of the art of shadow puppets. He experienced a moment's apprehension as he stepped inside the large tent – would this be a pale imitation of the artistry he remembered, an inept aping of the skills he had so admired in his younger days? He took his seat between a snotty-nosed girl and man who reeked of ale and was already snoring. But after a few moments, he noticed neither of them…

The ringing was so sustained and insistent that Carlisle assumed it must be either a creditor or a constable. It was therefore with some surprise that he found his master standing on the doorstep. Carlisle had rarely seen Mr Hapworth so distracted. He stood silhouetted against the pale glow of the snow-reflected moonlight, breathless and agitated.

'Thank you,' he muttered as he pushed past Carlisle and into the hallway.

'Are you quite well, sir?' the manservant felt compelled to ask.

'Well? Oh yes. But I have seen…' Hapworth shook his head. 'Things you could not countenance. What to do?' he wondered. 'Whatever to do?'

Hapworth lapsed into silence, standing at the foot of the stairs, as if uncertain whether to proceed up or not.

'There are some messages, sir,' Carlisle ventured, hoping to break Hapworth out of his unsettling reverie.

'Messages,' his master echoed. 'Yes, of course. A message. I must send a message at once and tell her what I have witnessed.'

'Sir?'

'Pen and ink.' Hapworth nodded vehemently. 'In my study. I shall set down exactly what has happened this afternoon, and then you must bear the epistle. At once.'

'Of course, sir. May I ask to whom this message must be delivered?'

Hapworth was already hurrying through to his study. Carlisle followed him into the large room. Each wall was lined with bookcases from floor to ceiling, interrupted only by a large window on one wall and the gas lamps that jutted out from between the shelves and cast a gentle luminance across the room. In the middle of the room was a large globe. To one side, Hapworth's desk. On the other, a small table bearing a decanter and glasses. Hapworth made straight for the desk, pulling a sheet of writing paper from a tray and setting it squarely on the blotter before reaching into a drawer for pen and ink.

'Sir,' Carlisle prompted. 'The letter you wish me to deliver? Who is it for?'

Hapworth glanced up. His eyes were shadowed, his cheeks hollow, his fingers trembling as he held the pen. 'Why, to the Great Detective, of course. To Madame Vastra.'

Carlisle shivered despite himself. He had been to Paternoster Row before. Hapworth was acquainted with Madame Vastra, and she had called upon his learning and knowledge on several occasions. Carlisle found the veiled woman cold and not a little unsettling.

'Now I must set this down at once,' Hapworth insisted. 'Leave me. I shall ring for you when I am done.'

As he spoke, Hapworth put down his pen and got to his feet, following Carlisle to the door. As soon as the manservant was out in the hall, Hapworth pulled the door shut. A moment later, Carlisle heard the scrape of the key turning in the lock. Only then did it occur to Carlisle that his master was utterly terrified.

Inside the study, Hapworth closed and barred the shutters on the window, then drew the curtains across. He took a moment to adjust the gas, turning up the lamps as he fought to get his nerves under control.

At his desk, he paused before sitting. He shrugged out of his coat and draped it across the globe. The last flecks of snow had melted, but a tiny patch of white was visible. Something poking out of the coat pocket. Hapworth lifted the coat to reach inside, and drew out the ticket he had been given when he entered the Carnival of Curiosities. It was damp and stained. As he pulled it from the coat pocket, several other, smaller pieces of paper came with it and scattered across the polished wooden floorboards. He bent to pick them up.

Three pieces of paper, snow white, each folded into the shape of a stylised bird. It was expertly done, all the more impressive as the birds were so small – only a couple of inches across. Hapworth dropped the paper birds, together with the Carnival ticket, beside the ornate letter-opener on his desk and sat down, gathering his thoughts before committing them to the paper in front of him.

A faint breeze ruffled the folded paper, giving the illusion for a moment that the wings of the birds were stirring into life. Hapworth glanced across at the window – only to see that, of course, it was closed, the shutters and curtains drawn. He frowned.

Outside the door, Carlisle waited, unsure quite what to do. He had no idea how long Mr Hapworth would be, but equally he did not want to venture too far away. His master might need him at any moment.

The scream echoed round the hallway, barely muffled by the heavy study door. It seemed to go on for ever, before it was choked off into a rasp of pain.

'Sir?' Carlisle called. 'Mr Hapworth?'

The door was still locked. Carlisle put his shoulder to it, and with a strength borne of fear and urgency he managed to break it open on his third attempt. He stumbled into the room, accompanied by the sound of splintering wood as the doorframe gave way.

Hapworth was still at his desk, but sprawled forward across it, his body twisted onto its side. One hand was stretched out desperately across the surface, fingers curled into a gnarled claw. His eyes were open, staring wide, fearful, and lifeless at Carlisle standing in the shattered doorway.

On the paper before him, Hapworth had written just two words: 'Madame Vastra'. The paper was flecked with red.

Carlisle looked round, appalled. But apart from him and Hapworth's body, the room was empty. The window was locked and shuttered. He had broken through the only door to get inside.

Blood continued to seep out from the sharp metal letter-opener that jutted from between Hapworth's shoulder blades. It dripped to the desk, soaked up by the crimson-stained blotter.

Chapter

I

The pub was crowded. People stood so close together that they were almost on each other's toes, except for at one end of the bar, where two stocky figures stood alone. There seemed to be an unspoken understanding that no one else should get too close to them.

Everything about Rick Bellamy was angry. His face was a permanent scowl, his hands – except when lifting his pint glass – knotted into fists, his stance pugilistic and intimidating. His tone was no exception.

'A penny!' He spat the word across the bar in front of him. 'Well, I thought, there must be something good in here, then. But no, it was just the usual rubbish for the punters. More stalls and sideshows and the like. Freaks and exhibits. Oh, interesting enough I s'pose. But a *penny*. Carnival of Curiosities? More like a rip-off.'

'Your anger does you credit,' Bellamy's companion said. 'I imagine you laid waste the entire area and demanded restitution.'

Bellamy drained his glass and slammed it down on the bar. 'Well no, actually,' he admitted. 'Though I did give them a piece of my mind. Told them what I thought. Made it clear how angry it made me. Then I put it down to experience and came here for a drink. You ready for another one, Mr Strax?'

'Allow me.' Mr Strax finished his own pint. Rather than set down the empty glass, he crushed it casually between his large fingers until it exploded into a satisfying spray of shards and fragments. 'Boy!' he called across the bar. 'Two more pints.'

The serving girl sighed, left the customer she was serving, and pulled the beers.

'You not working tonight, Mr Strax?' Bellamy asked as they waited for their drinks.

'My mistress was called away. I declined to join her. A swift strategic assessment suggested you would be here.'

'I appreciate the company,' Bellamy said, though his face was still clinging to its irate frown.

'And I find your perpetual ire refreshing. Most humans keep their wrath hidden away. We could have a fight later,' Strax added hopefully.

'Not tonight. I've had a few too many, I fancy. And I've a bare-knuckle match tomorrow afternoon. Come and watch if you like. Blackfriars.'

'Ah, sport!' Strax nodded. Since he had no neck to speak of, this involved moving most of his upper body. 'I may indeed. How many of these black friars will you kill?'

The pub was considerably less crowded by the time Strax and Bellamy finished their conversation. Strax, as he had said, found Bellamy a refreshing change from most humans in that his anger spilled out in every word and expression, every movement and action. Strax had never told Bellamy that he was not actually human himself, but was in fact a cloned warrior of the far superior Sontaran race temporarily working as manservant to a prehistoric lizard woman. But if he had, Bellamy would probably have nodded, swigged his drink, and complained about the state of the East End. Or the incompetence of the government. Or his poverty and current inability to find gainful employment. Or the price of the beer. The notion of friendship was alien to both of them, but if they had to enumerate their friends, then each would have been on the rather short list produced by the other.

In Bellamy's case, Strax might well have been the only name to feature.

'Maybe see you at Blackfriars tomorrow,' Bellamy said as they parted company outside the tavern.

'It is certainly a possibility,' Strax agreed. He slapped Bellamy on the back, making the big man stumble. Bellamy was a good head taller than Strax, and almost as broad – one of the few humans who could sustain a fight with Strax for more than a few seconds. 'I have fought against Headless Monks,' Strax told him, 'so a few black friars will pose little problem. We should meet beforehand to discuss a suitable strategy.'

'Whatever,' Bellamy agreed. 'G'night then.' He made a half-hearted attempt to return the slap on the back, which Strax barely noticed though it would have felled most people.

Strax watched Bellamy disappear into the distance, becoming little more than a shadow beneath the glow of the gas lamps. Then he turned and headed back towards Paternoster Row. There was snow in the air again, a few flakes lazily drifting down to land on his dark jacket. But Strax didn't mind the cold. His mind was already on the tasks he needed to perform when he got back. The surveillance systems would need to be primed. His personal blaster rifle could do with de-ionising and recharging. He would check the locks on the windows and doors for any sign of attempted entry. And there was the washing-up to do.

The cold of the night cleared Bellamy's head as he walked. The snow was getting heavier, starting to settle on the pavement and across his broad shoulders. The streets were quiet, but this being London they were rarely deserted. A late cab hurried past, the horse's hooves and the iron-clad wheels clattering on the cobbles. A woman with her face painted thick flashed a gap-toothed grin at Bellamy from the entrance to a narrow alleyway. He ignored her.

Further along, passing along the side of a large industrial building, the light from a gas lamp cast the shadow of a figure against the side wall of another narrow alley. The figure raised its hand and beckoned. Bellamy ignored this figure too.

Except…

He stopped, and turned back. He could see the shadow on the wall. He could see the lamp casting the light. But – whose shadow was it? There was no one there.

The shadow beckoned again, insistent. Then, as if assuming Bellamy would follow, it turned and walked down the alleyway. Still he could see no one, could hear no footsteps. He looked round to see if anyone else had remarked the shadow, but the street was empty. His face contorted into an even angrier expression, Bellamy gave in to his curiosity.

The alley was dark. But he could see the shadow, cast against the wall further along the narrow passageway. It hesitated, turned back, beckoned him onwards again. Whoever this joker was, he'd not find it so funny when Bellamy caught up with him. He'd tell the fellow what he thought about conjuring tricks like this, and in no uncertain terms.

Bellamy picked up his pace, striding swiftly after the shadow. The alley turned abruptly, running past the doors of a large building – an abandoned warehouse or factory. This part of the passageway was suffused with a pale yellow glow. There was a lamp at the end, where it emerged again onto a main street. Snowflakes twisted and danced through the light before settling on the cold ground. There was no sign of the shadow, or whoever had cast it.

Bellamy gave a grunt of anger, and turned to retrace his steps. As he turned, a man stepped out of the doorway of the large building, making Bellamy gasp in sudden surprise. It wasn't the figure that had cast the shadow, of that Bellamy was sure. This man was thinner, almost gaunt. Deep-set eyes and hollow cheeks. A narrow beak of a nose. And the long frock coat he wore was a distinctive shape, to say nothing of the black top hat. A swathe of dark material hung from the back of the hat. He might not have cast the shadow, but the man looked as if he had coalesced out of the darkness. Even his gloves were so black that they seemed to absorb light as he raised his hand in greeting.

'You want to be careful, creeping about like that,' Bellamy said. 'Here, did you see another bloke come this way?' he wondered.

'Only you.' The man's voice was deep and sonorous. His grim expression did not change.

'You look like you're on your way to a funeral,' Bellamy said.

Still the man's expression did not alter. 'And who says the illiterate have no sense of irony?'

Bellamy felt the anger rising in him. 'The what? Are you insulting me?' He took a step forward, fist raised.

A few moments later, the tall man dressed all in black walked slowly away down the alley. He paused for a moment, body braced as if he was about to sneeze. His expressionless face twisted into a sudden and extreme snarl of pure rage. Just for a second, then the anger faded again and the man's face settled back into its previous, neutral appearance.

On the ground behind him, Bellamy lay twisted and still. The clothes seemed far too big for the wizened, emaciated husk of a body. A skeletal hand stretched out across the ground, fleshless fingers frozen in the act of clawing desperately at the cobbles as if trying to cling to the last moments of fading life.

Chapter

2

'King Arthur.'

'No.'

Clara glared. 'What do you mean, "No"?'

The Doctor didn't look up from the TARDIS console, just put up his hand like a policeman stopping traffic. 'No. Not King Arthur.'

'You said I could choose.'

'Within reason.' He still didn't look up.

'Not what you said. I can choose, you said. Any place any time any person, you said. So I choose King Arthur.'

'No.'

'We just did that.'

'Still no.' He did look up now. His eyes were lost in shadow so it was hard for Clara to see if he was joking or deadly serious. The rest of his face always looked serious, it was the eyes that were the clue. If you could see them.

'So why not?'

'Not a good time, that's all.'

'You got something better to do?'

'The time of King Arthur is not a good time. Smelly, dirty, dangerous. You'd hate it. Besides…' He turned back to the console, cradling his chin in his hand as he stared at the screen.

'Besides?' Clara went over to join him, staring over his shoulder at the jumble of lines and squiggles and blobs on the screen. 'Besides what?'

The Doctor sighed, straightened up, and waved his hand at the screen. 'Well, look at it. Just look at it. There. See?'

'Um, no. Is it broken?'

That earned her a raised eyebrow.

'What then?'

'Power spike.'

'Something wrong with the TARDIS?'

'Not the TARDIS, no. A power spike in the late nineteenth century, right in the middle of London. Someone's using a post-nuclear power supply, and that's not good. Oh, they've got it shielded,' he went on, striding round the console, hands behind his back and head down as he considered. 'Which just confirms the fact that it can't be a natural phenomenon or an instrumental anomaly.'

'Well, quite. Late Victorian London?'

'That's what I said.'

'Could it be Madame Vastra? Maybe Strax is messing

about with some new post-nuclear weapon.'

'Very likely he is. But no.' The Doctor shook his head. 'No, no, no. They'd never be that careless. This is someone who doesn't want to be found, but who has no idea of the anachronistic implications.'

'So we forget King Arthur and go and sort out this post-nuclear spike, is that what you're suggesting?'

He was already working the controls. 'It wasn't a suggestion.' He glanced across at Clara. 'We'd better get changed into something that blends in a little more, don't you think?'

'You already look Victorian,' she told him.

'"We" was a tactful term. It wasn't actually me I was talking about.'

'That's a first.' Clara looked down at her bright blue blouse and short skirt. Maybe he had a point. 'I'll find something that will fit in with late Victorian then.'

He was working the controls again, pulling a lever and checking a dial. 'Choose something practical. It'll be smelly, dirty and dangerous,' he warned her. 'You'll love it.'

Frost clung to the trees like brittle blossom. The snow was filmed with a thick crust where it had frozen over. Icicles looked as if they had sprouted from the undersides of windowsills and ledges. Most impressive of all, the wide expanse of the river Thames was a sheet of opaque ice.

'There's a definite nip in the air,' the Doctor observed.

Clara's breath misted in front of her. 'You can say that again. Well, not actually say it again,' she added quickly. He could be so literal sometimes.

The TARDIS had landed in a narrow, deserted street close to the river. Judging by the lack of footprints in the snow, it was not a street that saw a lot of traffic.

'So, have you got some instrument that can lead us to this power source?' Clara asked as they set off along the pavement beside the river.

'Power *spike*. It's not a source, it was a spike, a spike that came from a source.'

'Which is different, right?'

'Right. And because it was a spike, it just happened the once. So now it's gone, and there's nothing to detect.'

'Unless it does it again?'

'Unless it does it again. In which case…' He pulled the sonic screwdriver from his pocket and checked its settings. 'In which case we'll know. But we can't just wait for it to happen, because it might not.'

'So how do we find this power source, then?'

'We investigate. The TARDIS landed us as close as she could, but we could still be a couple of miles away.'

'Oh, is that all?'

'That's not bad over several centuries and few million light years. Anyway, it shouldn't be too hard to track down an alien presence in London. Chances are that they'll be obvious, arrogant, think themselves superior.'

Clara gave the Doctor a good stare. 'Yeah, right.'

His eyebrows knitted together. 'What are you implying?'

'Nothing,' she said quickly. 'So, what's the plan? Pop along to Paternoster Row and ask our local friends for help?'

'Vastra and Strax and Jenny? Oh no, we don't need to bother them. Trust me.' He shook his head. 'This'll be easy.'

It was late morning and a steady stream of people made their way to the Frost Fair. Caught up in the tide, Clara and the Doctor were happy to go with the flow.

'So, it's not desperately urgent, this power spike?' Clara said through a mouthful of roasted chestnuts.

The Doctor was examining a baked potato, trying to work out how best to attack it. 'We're investigating,' he said, before taking a huge bite. He hopped from foot to foot, mouth open, and gasping.

'Hot?' Clara guessed.

The Doctor nodded furiously, while also somehow managing to scowl at a nearby boy who was laughing at the spectacle.

'I think you just wanted an excuse not to go and see King Arthur.'

'Not at all.' He blew furiously on what was left of the steaming potato. 'Though last time I visited there was a bit of a problem with a sword.'

'Really?'

'He was very young at the time, came running up shouting that he needed a sword, so I handed it to him.'

'And that was a problem.'

The Doctor risked some more potato. 'Apparently,' he said as he chewed, 'Arthur was supposed to take the sword out of the stone *himself*. Lot of fuss about nothing, if you ask me. But I did get to be King of England for a day before I abdicated in his favour. No real harm done. Are you going to stand here chattering all day?'

'Sorry.'

'What's that over there?' He didn't wait for an answer, but popped the rest of the potato in his mouth and strode off into the crowds.

The centrepiece of the fair was a large merry-go-round. Clara watched the horses rising and falling as they spun. Coupled with the music there was an almost hypnotic quality to the scene. The Doctor watched with her for a few minutes, then dived off on his own, and they met again by a stall selling rag dolls and cloth purses.

'You having fun, love?' the woman at the stall asked.

'Oh yes,' Clara assured her, hoping she had said

it loud enough to cover the Doctor's less positive response. 'Is there a fortune teller?' she asked on a whim.

'That'll be in the Carnival.'

'The Carnival?'

The woman pointed. 'Up that end is the Carnival of Curiosities. They've got all sorts in there. It'll cost you a penny each to get in, mind.'

'Want to give it a go?' Clara asked the Doctor.

'Oh yes. It sounds…'

'Curious?'

He smiled. 'Intriguing.'

The Doctor produced two shiny pennies to pay at the gate into the Carnival of Curiosities, receiving two cardboard tickets in return.

'Just show this if you want to come back later today, squire,' the lad on the gate told him. 'Only valid for today though, mind. Tickets'll be a different colour tomorrow.'

Inside the enclosure, there was an open area where several stalls were set up in the snow, and tents round the outside. The fortune teller was something of a disappointment. The elderly woman, wrapped in a shawl, sat at a table hunched over a crystal ball. She waggled her fingers over it, having first deprived Clara of another halfpenny, then gave a bored and obviously pretty standard spiel about her meeting a tall handsome stranger and going on a long journey.

'Well that much is right, I suppose,' she said to the Doctor. 'You want a go?'

He shook his head. 'Either she's a charlatan, in which case there's no point. Or she genuinely can see into the future in which case meeting me will probably provoke a coronary.'

He was more interested in an exhibition of 'Never-Creatures'. Once inside the tent, they found themselves confronted with glass bell jars filled with unidentifiable organic matter and grotesque sculptures. Labels suggested the contents were anything from a still-born starchild to a breed of moon-pig only found in the mountains of Spain.

The prize exhibit, stretched out under a glass case at the end of the tent was a dead mermaid. The Doctor spared it little more than a glance. 'An obvious fake,' he announced, just too loudly for comfort. 'The skin's the wrong colour and those fins are entirely the wrong shape.'

He embarrassed Clara again by yawning loudly in the middle of the Strong Man's demonstration outside the tent. The man was huge, his upper body covered with tattoos that included a dagger on each bicep and chains across his chest. With his bald head and broad physique he reminded Clara a little of Strax, except the man was much taller – well over six feet. He impressed the rest of his audience by smashing a pile of bricks with his hand, breaking a slab of stone with his forehead, and finally attempting to lift a metal pole with baskets of rocks attached at each end.

The muscles in his neck and arms stood out impressively as he strained and grunted and eventually managed to raise the rocks off the ground. He braced his legs, hefted the pole to his chest, and staggered as he struggled to lift it high above his head.

The Doctor sighed, looking round to see if there was anything more interesting happening somewhere else.

'You got a problem, mister?' the Strong Man demanded, slowly lowering the pole. He kept it braced across his chest as he stared at the Doctor.

'Me?'

'That's right – you.'

'Sorry.' The Doctor walked up to the Strong Man. 'I just wasn't *that* impressed, I'm afraid.'

'Really?'

'Doctor,' Clara warned.

There was a tangible air of anticipation among the crowd as the Strong Man glared back at the Doctor. 'I can soon teach you to be impressed.'

'You think so?' The Doctor gave Clara a 'What can you do?' glance. Then he took the metal pole from the man, holding it easily in one hand, steady as the rocks in the baskets attached to each end. 'Let me hold that while you try.'

The Strong Man stared back, astonished.

'What's your name?' the Doctor asked.

'Michael.'

'Michael what?'

'Michael, sir.'

'No, no, no. Let me put this down.' The Doctor set down the pole carefully. 'What's your surname? Michael what?'

'Oh. Michael Smith.'

'Ah!' The Doctor's face cracked into a sudden smile. 'I'm a Smith myself. Doctor John Smith, well sort of. Us Smiths have to stick together, you know. Good act, by the way. Maybe work on your presentation a bit. Develop some patter to keep people interested.'

'Yes,' Michael the Strong Man said. 'Thank you, sir.'

The Doctor turned away. 'No problem. Oh,' he said, looking back for a moment, 'and try to make it look difficult.'

'I have never been more embarrassed in my entire life,' Clara told him as they walked away, ignoring the stares of the crowd.

'Yes you have.'

'Yes I have,' she admitted. 'But I was probably with you at the time.'

The last tent they visited, right at the back of the enclosure, advertised 'The Most Magickal Shadowplay.'

'If it was that impressive,' the Doctor said, 'they'd

be able to spell "magical".'

'Don't be so grumpy and come and enjoy the show,' Clara told him.

The show was already in progress, so they made their way to the nearest seats at the back of the darkened tent. Across the tops of the heads of the rest of the audience, Clara stared transfixed at the screen. The principle was simple. A light was shone from behind the thin screen, and cut-out puppets between light and screen cast shadows as the show unfolded. There didn't seem to be a story as such, not in this part of the show anyway. It was more of a display, a dance of animals, of flights of birds, of figures so lifelike and so well animated that it was easy to believe the shadows were real, were *alive*.

'It's good, isn't it,' the Doctor whispered. It was a refreshing change to find he was actually impressed. 'Is it just me,' he added, 'or is it actually impossible?'

'What do you mean?' Clara hissed back. 'Can't you just enjoy it?'

'Oh I can, I am. But…'

'But? But *what*?'

'But, they're puppets.'

'Obviously.' She turned back to watch the show. A butterfly fluttered delicately through the air, chased by a child with a net. Her mind had no problem filling the dark shadows with imaginary texture, detail and colour.

'So,' the Doctor whispered right in her ear, 'where are the strings, or the rods? If they're puppets – what keeps them up and makes them move?'

Clara frowned. Actually he was right. 'Well, they're hidden, that's all,' she decided. 'Or the wires are extremely thin. It's very clever.'

'I wouldn't argue with that.'

The show ended to a riot of applause. The screen rose into the air, to reveal a figure standing behind. A young woman wearing a red cloak. The hood was folded back, so that her long hair spilled down the back – black as shadows. Her features were delicate, almost childlike, as she took a bow.

She was still standing there as the tent emptied. Clara turned to go, and found that the Doctor was already hurrying the other way, down to where the woman stood.

'How do you do it?' he was demanding as she arrived.

'Sorry,' Clara said before the woman could reply. 'What he meant to say was: "That was really impressive and we enjoyed it very much."'

The woman shook Clara's hand, and smiled. 'I'm glad my show entertained you.'

'It did,' the Doctor agreed. 'So, like I said, how do you do it?'

'This is the Doctor, by the way,' Clara said. 'And I'm Clara.'

'I have always had a talent for shadow puppetry,' the woman said. 'For bringing shadows and shapes to life. You'll forgive me if I don't share all my secrets with you. My skill is all that I have.'

'I'm sure that's not true,' the Doctor said. 'But like Clara said – impressive. Thank you. Oh,' he added as they turned to go, 'you didn't tell us your name.'

The woman pulled the hood of her cloak up over her head, so that her face fell into shadow. A striking red figure standing stark against the glow of the lamp at the back of the tent.

'I am Silhouette,' she said.

Chapter

3

'I still don't think it's possible,' the Doctor said as they made their way back through the fair.

'Just because you don't understand it,' Clara told him. 'Tell you what, why don't we agree that it's magic? That covers it.'

He fixed her with a stare that was somewhere between sympathetic and condescending. 'Magic is just a term people use for things they're too primitive to understand properly.'

Clara nodded. 'I think that's what I just said, actually.'

They paused to watch a man in a short cape and impressive moustache doing card tricks. He fanned out the pack and waved it at the Doctor.

'Pick a card. Any card. Don't tell me what it is, but show it to the young lady there, and then to everyone else.'

The Doctor showed everyone his card – the three of diamonds.

'Good, now replace it in the pack, anywhere you like. That's it.'

The conjuror shuffled the pack. Then he cut it. Then he shuffled it again. Finally, he threw the pack up into the air. One card separated from the others, and he caught it in one hand. The rest of the pack, he caught in the other.

'And tell me, sir,' he announced confidently, 'if this is your card?'

The crowd was silent. The Doctor peered at the card. The seven of clubs. 'No, it's not.'

The conjuror's smile became rather more fixed as he quickly looked through the rest of the cards. 'All part of the trick,' he said rather unconvincingly. 'Ah! Queen of spades.'

'No.'

'Nine of hearts?'

'Still no.'

The conjuror sniffed and frowned. 'So what was it?'

'Left pocket,' the Doctor told him.

The conjuror's frown deepened as he pulled an unexpected card from his trouser pocket. 'Three of diamonds?'

'That's the one. Sorry, I cheated.'

They headed back through the Carnival towards the main Frost Fair. The snow was getting heavier, settling on top of the compacted snow already lying on the ground.

'So what's the plan now?' Clara asked.

'Jenny,' the Doctor told her.

'Clara,' she corrected him. 'Remember?'

'Jenny Flint, Vastra's maid, is over there,' he told her. 'Coincidence, do you think?'

As they approached they saw that Jenny was talking to Michael the Strong Man. 'Elderly gent, with white hair and mutton-chop whiskers,' she was saying.

Michael shook his head. 'Sorry. Don't remember him. But we get so many people through here in a day. He could have been here, couldn't say for sure. I doubt if I remember even half of them.' He glanced across as the Doctor and Clara arrived. 'I remember Doctor Smith here, though.'

'Doctor Smith?' Jenny turned, surprised. 'Oh yeah. Everyone knows Doctor Smith.'

Michael excused himself and headed off to do another performance.

'So what brings you to the Carnival of Curiosities?' Jenny asked.

'Curiosity,' the Doctor told her.

'Ask a silly question. Between you and me,' she went on, 'it ain't that curious. I've seen better. You looked at that mermaid they've got?' She shook her head. 'Hopeless.'

'Maybe they should get a Lizard Woman,' Clara suggested.

'Be a darn sight better than the Wolf Boy over there.

You seen him?' They confessed they hadn't. 'He just needs a good bath, he does. I asked him if he was all right, when the woman what's in charge wasn't looking, and he asked me if I could get him a meat pie. Polite as you like. Even said please. Wolf Boy, my elbow.'

'So what are you doing here?' the Doctor asked. 'Apart from being singularly unimpressed with just about everything.'

'Looking for a man with mutton-chop whiskers, by the sound of it,' Clara added.

'Marlowe Hapworth is his name. But I know where he is now, right enough.'

'Then why are you asking about him?' Clara wondered.

'Because he's dead is where he is. It's *how* he died as makes no sense.'

'A case for the Great Detective,' the Doctor guessed.

Jenny nodded. 'Found a ticket to this Carnival on Hapworth's desk. From the colour, it's yesterday's. That's when he died. His manservant says he came home in a fluster, locked himself in his study, and a few minutes later he's dead. Stabbed with a letter-opener.'

'Suicide?' Clara suggested.

'Not unless he was a contortionist. The letter-opener was shoved in between his shoulder blades.'

'And I take it the room had no other obvious

entrance?' the Doctor said.

'One window, locked and with the shutters across.'

'So the police called in Madame Vastra,' Clara guessed.

'No, the dead man did.'

'How's that possible?' Clara wondered.

'He was writing a letter to her when he was killed. Carlisle, that's his butler, says he came back from a walk all anxious like and worried and said he had to tell Madame Vastra something important. Got as far as writing her name on the paper, and then someone put his lights out. For good.'

'So you're here to try to find out what upset him,' Clara said.

'If it was something here at all,' the Doctor pointed out. 'It could have been in the Frost Fair, or anywhere else on his walk.'

Jenny nodded. 'I've been retracing his route, best I can. But I ain't found nothing yet. This place is the most likely for something weird going on, though. And talking of "weird", you ain't told me why you're here yet.'

They were walking back through the Frost Fair now, having left the Carnival of Curiosities behind. The Doctor led the way to a large tent where tea was being served and they found a table in a secluded corner. Once they were settled and tea was ordered, he gave a brief explanation of the power spike.

'Don't know nothing about that,' Jenny said.

'Could be coincidence,' Clara added, through a mouthful of fruitcake.

'Possibly,' the Doctor conceded. 'You two carry on here,' he decided, 'see if you can piece together the unfortunate Mr Hapworth's final hours.'

'Where are you off to?' Clara asked.

The Doctor drained his tea and stood up. 'I'll go and talk to Vastra. See what she's discovered. Is she still at Hapworth's?'

'She is,' Jenny confirmed. 'Isn't there something else you need to ask me?' she said as the Doctor stood up.

'I don't think so. I find it best to keep an open mind, unclouded by the opinions of others. I shall inspect the scene of the crime and formulate my own opinion based on my own observations.'

'Right you are.' Jenny sipped her tea. 'Sure you don't have just one question?'

'Quite sure. I'll see you later, either back here or at Hapworth's house, or failing that back at Paternoster Row.'

He didn't wait for agreement, but set off between the tables towards the mouth of the tent.

'What do you reckon?' Jenny said. 'About thirty seconds?'

'A bit less,' Clara thought.

Just before he reached the entrance, the Doctor swung round and strode back towards them.

'All right,' he said as he reached the table. 'One more question. What's Hapworth's address?'

'So, you been busy since we last visited?' Clara wondered when the Doctor had gone again. It was warmer in the tent and she was in no hurry to finish her tea and cake.

'Pretty much. But nothing too exciting. We did have a haunted house to investigate last month. Poltergeist breaking plates and making the chandeliers swing about.'

'That sounds exciting,' Clara told her, thinking back to the haunted house she had visited with the Doctor not all that long ago and shivering at the memory.

'Nah. Turned out it was built on top of the Bakerloo Line and whenever a train went underneath it made the place shake.'

Clara laughed. 'And how's Strax?'

Jenny smiled. 'Same as ever, I'm sorry to say. He's off doing his own investigation at the moment.'

'Wearing an inverness cape and deerstalker hat?'

'Mercifully not. Some drinking partner of his got bumped off last night and he's taken umbrage.'

Clara put down her teacup. 'I'm not surprised. A pub brawl or something?'

'Sounds a bit more peculiar than that. But Strax didn't say much about it, except he's going to find the culprit and do something nasty to them involving coronic acid and scissor grenades.'

Finding a murderer had turned out not to be quite as easy as Strax had hoped and expected. He had learned a lot from his interrogation of local inhabitants, employing a level of subtlety that he felt Madame Vastra would have been proud of. He had killed no one, hadn't even threatened torture – well, except to that rude urchin who tried to remove Strax's wallet from his jacket pocket. He wouldn't try that again in a hurry. Even when his fingers were better.

But what Strax had learned did not reassure him. The local police were not terribly forthcoming, even when Strax mentioned Vastra's name. But Inspector Goodwin had let slip that Rick Bellamy was not the first victim.

A sympathetic pathologist, who seemed to be labouring under the misconception that Strax was suffering from some sort of physiological disorder, was more helpful.

'Quite desiccated,' he explained. 'It's as if his entire body was drained of everything that made the poor man what he is. Left behind a withered husk that was only identified by the contents of his wallet. Surprised the murderer left that behind, not that there was much money in it.'

'Could it be a case of death from natural causes?' Strax wondered. He hoped not.

'If we had just one instance of such a condition then I might agree with you. But no, this poor fellow – like all the others – was killed quite deliberately. But as to how or by whom, well, I have to confess I'm rather stumped.'

Having obtained a list of the victims' names and addresses, Strax attempted to find a common thread that linked them. There was none. A landlady, a publican, a brother, and a young woman called Maud (who seemed to have no concept of personal space and was altogether so familiar that Strax suspected she was involved in some form of personal espionage) all painted very different pictures of the victims. They were different ages, from different areas – though all rather deprived – and some were apparently female.

The only thing they seemed to have in common, Strax reflected as he made his way through the East End streets, was that they were down on their luck and none too pleased about it. Strax imagined they would all have got on rather well with Bellamy, swapping stories about how awful or expensive or generally unpleasant everything was.

Strax needed time to reflect on what he had discovered. Perhaps he would consult Jenny or Vastra and see what they thought. But first he would inspect the scene of the latest crime. He knew Bellamy's body had been removed as he had been allowed a glimpse of it at the morgue, so the unhelpful police should have moved on. It did not look as if the poor man had enjoyed an honourable death – all the more reason to avenge him. So muttering angrily to himself, he made his way towards where Bellamy had been found.

Strax found the narrow alleyway where the body had been discovered in the early hours. His shoulders almost touched the walls on either side as he reached a large building that seemed to be abandoned and derelict. Ahead of him, a figure stepped out of a shadowy doorway. He was dressed in a sort of ritual apparel that Strax had seen before – all black, with a tall helmet on top of his head, a swathe of dark material hanging from the back. Strax seemed to recall that personnel in this sort of uniform were responsible for the removal and burial of the dead.

'Your client has already been removed,' Strax announced helpfully.

The man's face did not move. 'You seem angry about something,' he said, his voice deep and dark.

Strax considered this. 'No,' he decided. 'I am on a mission to avenge the death of a colleague. There is nothing more honourable or satisfying.'

The man took a few steps closer, and Strax himself also approached, stepping out of the shadows and into the pale winter sunlight for the first time.

The man stopped as he saw Strax properly for the first time. He reached up and touched the brim of his tall hat. 'I beg your pardon, sir,' he said. 'If you will excuse me, I have business elsewhere.'

Somehow he squeezed past Strax and continued down the alleyway. Strax turned to watch him go. But all he saw was a fading shadow on the end wall.

Chapter

4

It seemed likely that Hapworth had visited the Frost Fair as well as the Carnival of Curiosities. Indeed, he must have passed through it to get to the Carnival in the first place. The fair was big, stretched out across the bank of the Thames, with some stalls and attractions on the frozen river itself. It made sense for Jenny and Clara to split up to cover as much of it as they could.

Jenny gave Clara a good description of Hapworth. 'If we know where he went and who and what he saw, we might get a clue to what upset him before he headed home,' she said. 'Though it might not be anything here at all, of course.'

'Won't know till we find out, though, will we?' Clara said. 'I'll meet you back at the tea tent. That's probably where the Doctor will look for us too.'

It was her feet that got coldest. Trudging through the snow as it turned to slush beneath the feet of so many other people, Clara could feel the chill eating through the soles of her boots. There was no sign of Jenny in the crowds, and Clara couldn't honestly say she was making much progress. She had found several people who definitely remembered Marlowe Hapworth from yesterday. But none of them could recall anything remarkable about him or his behaviour or demeanour. There were others who thought that perhaps they had seen him, but could not be sure. But none of them could offer anything much of interest about an elderly man apparently enjoying the Frost Fair on a bright, crisp winter's afternoon.

They had not really agreed a time to meet back at the tea tent, but Clara assumed it would take Jenny about as long to cover the half of the fair she had taken as Clara took to go round hers. So as soon as she was done she headed back. The tent was crowded now, and she had to wait for a table to become free.

Clara was still deciding whether she wanted anything to eat along with her cup of tea when someone cleared their throat politely beside her.

'Excuse me?'

She looked up to see a young man, about her own age, standing with his hand resting on the back of one of the chairs.

'Do you mind terribly if I join you?' he asked. 'Only it's rather crowded at the moment.' He smiled. 'I'm sorry, if you're expecting company then of course I shall look for another table.'

'No, no,' Clara said quickly. 'Please do join me. I'm

meeting a friend but she might be a while yet. So I'd be glad of the company.'

'You're very kind.' He sat down opposite Clara, and smiled.

Clara couldn't help but smile back. The man seemed polite and self-assured. His dark hair was combed back from his rather handsome face. As he turned to wave to a waitress, Clara saw that his nose turned up just very slightly at the end, rather as her own did.

'What can I order for you?' he asked as a waitress approached. 'The toasted tea cakes are very good.'

Clara found she quite fancied a toasted tea cake now he mentioned it.

'Please, let this be my treat,' he said as the waitress departed again. 'In return for your generously sharing your table with me. I'm sorry, I haven't even asked your name and here I am buying you tea cake.'

'Clara.'

'How do you do, Miss Clara.'

She laughed. 'No, just Clara will do.'

'How informal. Then please, I am Oswald.'

'Oswald?'

His smile faded. 'You don't like the name?'

'No, I'm surprised that's all.'

'I didn't realise it was a surprising name.'

'*My* name is also Oswald,' she explained. 'Clara Oswald.'

'It seems we have a lot in common then – our names and a penchant for toasted tea cakes.'

Oswald was pleasant company and easy to speak to. The tea cakes were indeed very good, and Clara found herself laughing and enjoying the company. Oswald turned out to be tutor to several children, and was impressed to discover that Clara was herself a teacher, though he seemed slightly confused as to why she wasn't in school today. She managed to gloss over that, and found herself telling him more than she had intended about herself. She told him that she had travelled extensively, but kept the details vague.

'Your friend is a long time,' Oswald said as they ordered another pot of tea. 'I do hope she hasn't been detained.'

'Jenny'll be here,' Clara assured him. 'And the Doctor too.'

'Doctor? You're not unwell, I hope?'

'No. Another friend.'

'A very good friend, I imagine from the way you say that.'

'Yes,' she agreed. 'We have travelled together to, well, all sorts of places. He's become a bit more grumpy recently,' she found herself admitting. 'He's got, well, *older*, I suppose.'

'Happens to us all.'

It was strange, Clara thought as the new pot of tea arrived, she had only known this man for a few minutes but already it seemed like they were good friends. It was like she'd known Oswald for years. Several times when she hesitated, he seemed to know what she had been about to say. Seemed to sense how she felt. It was very easy to be in his company, she decided. And the fact that he was also very easy on the eye helped of course... She smiled and nodded as he offered to refill her cup.

Madame Vastra lowered her veil as she heard the study door open behind her. She turned from the bookcase she had been examining, and was surprised to see the Doctor standing in the doorway. She raised her veil again and nodded a greeting.

The Doctor strode in, pushing the door closed behind him. 'Scene of the crime?' he asked.

Vastra indicated Hapworth's desk. 'He was found slumped forward, the letter-opener in his back.'

There was still blood on the desktop and soaked into the blotter. Dark splashes surrounded the chair.

'The police removed the body, and still have the letter-opener,' Vastra explained. 'They are, as seems to be the natural state of the police, baffled.'

The Doctor nodded thoughtfully. 'I was speaking to Hapworth's man, Carlisle. He says the door was locked and there's no other way in or out. Is that right?'

'Unless Carlisle is lying about the door. But he

seems truthful enough, and not a little upset.'

'Distraught, even,' the Doctor agreed.

'The window was locked and shuttered. The lock is secure, with no signs of it being forced.'

'Hidden doorway?' the Doctor suggested. 'Bookcases can conceal a variety of sins.'

'Not in this case, so far as I can ascertain.'

'So what do the police think, aside from being baffled?'

'They have decided that it must be either suicide or a bizarre accident, under the circumstances. They are therefore happy for me to investigate.'

'Well it saves them the effort. *Could* it be suicide?' he wondered.

'No.'

'Or an accident?'

'Unlikely. I saw the body *in situ*. He was stabbed in the middle of the back. He could not have reached to do it himself. As you can see, there is nowhere in the back of the chair where the blade could have been fixed either by accident or design for the poor man to fall back against and impale himself in such a manner.'

Vastra returned to her examination of the bookcases while the Doctor looked over the desk. A blood-stained sheet of writing paper bore the beginnings of a letter – just the salutation: 'Madame Vastra'.

'He was writing to me,' she explained, seeing

where the Doctor was looking. 'In a state of agitation, according to Carlisle. I did know Hapworth, though more in the nature of an acquaintance than as a friend. He was a man of learning, and his knowledge has proved useful in the past.'

'Jenny said you knew him.'

Vastra nodded. 'You have seen Jenny. That explains how you come to be here. You were at the Frost Fair?'

'The Carnival of Curiosities.' He picked up the cardboard ticket from beside the blotter. 'And this is the only clue you have found that might explain where he had been or what had upset him?'

'That and the three small birds.'

The Doctor frowned, his eyebrows knitting together. 'Birds? What birds?'

'Oh not real birds.' Vastra turned from the bookcase. 'They are made from paper, folded into the shape of a bird. Three of them. Rather stylised, quite clever.'

'Origami, you mean?'

'Do I?'

'Japanese for "folded paper", though thinking about it the word won't be used much around here for another sixty years yet.' He lifted the blotter to look underneath, then moved the wooden rack containing paper and envelopes. 'So where are these origami birds?'

Vastra walked over to join him. 'That's strange,' she

said, looking down at the desk. 'They were just there, beside the carnival ticket. I wonder where they went.'

The Doctor shrugged. 'Probably not important.' He smiled. 'It's good to see you again, Vastra. And don't worry about the birds. They must be around somewhere. They can't have flown away.'

Chapter

5

There was still no sign of Jenny when Clara and Oswald had finished their second pot of tea. Oswald consulted a pocket watch and apologised that he would have to be leaving.

'Thank you for allowing me to share your table,' he said as he stood up.

'No problem,' Clara told him. 'Thanks for the company.' She watched Oswald as he navigated his way towards the exit, smiling politely as he passed people and standing aside to allow others to get past. He really was very pleasant company, she thought.

Oswald had almost reached the way out when he stopped. Another man had just come in, and was approaching Oswald rapidly. They evidently knew each other, and after exchanging a few words, Oswald turned and nodded towards Clara. Perhaps the man was his employer – he looked like a 'gentleman of means'. She hoped she hadn't got Oswald into trouble by distracting him for too long.

The two of them – Oswald, together with the other man – were heading back through the tent towards Clara. As he approached, she could make out details of the man's appearance. He was perhaps 40, with receding dark hair and a short beard. A slight man, wearing a dark overcoat and carrying a silver-topped cane, which he raised in greeting as he arrived at the table.

'Forgive me, Clara,' Oswald said, 'but I just had to introduce you to my employer, Mr Milton.'

'I haven't got you into trouble, have I?' Clara asked quickly.

'Good gracious me, no,' Milton replied. His voice was slightly nasal and drawn out tight. 'When Oswald told me he'd been taking tea with a delightful young lady, also of the name of Oswald albeit her surname, I simply had to introduce myself. Orestes Milton, at your service, Miss Oswald.'

Clara felt her face colour slightly as Milton bowed his head and extended his hand. She shook it politely. 'Delighted to meet you, Mr Milton.'

Oswald excused himself, and headed off again.

'He's a good man,' Milton said, watching him go.

'He tutors your children, I gather,' Clara said.

'Ah, no. Now there you are incorrect.' Milton made a show of consulting his own watch. 'I must be getting along in a minute, but if I may sit for just a moment?'

'Please.'

'Thank you.' Milton seated himself across the small table from Clara. 'I am his employer, yes, but only in that I pay for his services. He teaches the children of the poor and attends the local workhouse.'

'And you pay for that?'

'I have been very fortunate in life, Miss Oswald,' Milton told her. 'I believe that one should give back to the community what one can.'

The chair beside Clara was suddenly pulled back and a figure slumped down untidily in it. 'What a very enlightened philosophy,' the Doctor said. 'Mind if I join you? Good. I'm sorry – I didn't catch your name?'

'Milton, sir. And you are, I assume the gentleman Miss Oswald has been waiting for?'

'Probably.' He reached across the table to shake hands. 'I'm the Doctor, Mr Milton. It's a pleasure.'

'Likewise. Though as I was explaining to Miss Oswald, a pleasure all too short as I am afraid I have business elsewhere.'

'Shame,' the Doctor said, leaning back and regarding Milton with interest. 'What sort of business, may I ask?'

'I am an industrialist, I suppose for want of a better word. We are pioneering a new process at one of my factories and I need to debrief the shift manager.'

The Doctor nodded as if this made the most perfect sense to him. 'Very wise. It's good to pay attention to the details of things, I find.'

'Indeed.' Milton rose to his feet. 'As a medical man, I see that you appreciate the importance of detail and accuracy.'

'Oh, I'm not that sort of doctor.'

'Oh? A doctor of divinity, perhaps?' Milton's lips twitched as he said it, suggesting he was being less than serious.

'Perhaps,' the Doctor said. 'I'm a doctor of so many things I forget more than half of them.'

'A man of intellect and learning, then.'

'He's certainly that,' Clara agreed, feeling she ought to get a word in at least.

'But at the moment, I'm an investigator,' the Doctor went on, as if she hadn't spoken.

'Really? How intriguing. Investigating what, may I ask?'

'Murder. Intrigue. And missing origami birds.'

'Missing what?' Clara said. This was news to her.

It was Milton who answered: 'Origami is the ancient Japanese art of paper-folding.'

'I know,' Clara said. 'It wasn't the vocabulary that surprised me.'

'Do you speak fluent Japanese, Mr Milton?' the Doctor asked. He was leaning forward across the table, looking up at the standing man with a studied intensity.

Milton smiled. 'Alas, not a word.'

'Pity.'

'And a pity too that I must leave.' Milton nodded to Clara, and reached out to shake the Doctor's hand. 'It has been most stimulating. I do hope we meet again.'

The Doctor waited until Milton had reached the exit from the tent then leapt to his feet. 'Time we were off.'

'Where to?'

The Doctor looked at her as if she was mad. 'To follow him, of course. Remind me how you know the philanthropic Mr Milton.'

'I don't,' Clara said as she hurried after him. 'I shared my table with a man who works for him. Or at least, he's funded by him. Why?'

'Because Milton is a man out of time, that's why.'

They reached the mouth of the tent and the Doctor scanned the surrounding Frost Fair until he spotted his quarry heading off in the direction of the Carnival of Curiosities. 'Ah – there he goes. Come on.'

'What do you mean, "a man out of time"? Is he a time traveller like us?'

'Not necessarily. He might just have an over sophisticated translation morpher.'

'A what?'

'Makes it look and sound like he's speaking your language so you can understand him.

'We could anyway, couldn't we? Because of the TARDIS?'

The Doctor paused to give Clara a withering look.

'Yes, but he doesn't know that. And I doubt if he had it installed for our benefit.'

They showed their tickets at the gate, and hurried through into the Carnival to see where Milton had gone. There was no sign of the man.

'He must have gone further in,' the Doctor decided. 'Walking quickly, so a man with a purpose and a precise destination.'

'Something here he's keen to see, maybe.'

'Something, or someone,' the Doctor agreed as they hurried through the Carnival.

Clara spotted him first. 'There he is,' she said, pointing to where Milton was just disappearing behind the Shadowplay tent. 'So, you could tell all that stuff about him using a translator or whatever just by looking at him, could you?'

'I could tell that by *listening* to him,' the Doctor said. 'He fell into my origami trap.'

'And how does that translate into Earth-Speak? I assume you don't mean you constructed a net or something out of paper.'

'He used the word "debrief", meaning to get a report after the event. Which is all well and good but that particular Americanism won't be coined until towards the end of the Second World War. Could have been a quirk of our own translation system, so I mentioned origami. And he not only understood it, he gave us a definition. But the Japanese word doesn't enter the English language until, I think, the 1950s.'

'That's why you asked him if he spoke Japanese,' Clara realised.

'Can't keep you fooled for long.'

'Hey,' she said, realising something else. 'Maybe this Milton bloke is responsible for the power spike thingy we detected.'

The Doctor paused mid-step to look back at her. 'Oh, do you think?'

Clara ignored his sarcasm, pulling him back out of sight. 'He's coming back,' she warned. 'That was quick,' she added as Milton passed close by. He didn't seem to spot them in amongst the other people. 'I guess he didn't find what he was looking for.'

'Or perhaps he did,' the Doctor said.

They waited a few moments to let Milton get a good way ahead of them, but not so far there was a risk of losing sight of him. The woman from the shadow puppet show, Silhouette, appeared briefly at the opening to the tent close by, putting out a sign saying the next show would be in an hour's time. She smiled at Clara before disappearing back inside the tent.

'Probably taking a late lunch,' Clara thought.

'Right, off we go.' The Doctor took Clara's elbow and marched her after Milton. 'Looks like he's leaving again.'

Milton was already hurrying through the Frost Fair and back towards the Embankment. The Doctor and

Clara followed him as he turned off down a side street, then almost immediately into another. This street was deserted. The terraced houses looked dark and empty. Several had their windows boarded up. The paintwork was flaking and the stone was crumbling through neglect and the combined effects of the weather and the London smog.

They drew back into the shadows on the other side of the street as Milton paused outside one of the houses. He turned, looking back to check that he was unobserved. Then he walked up to the front door.

'Doesn't look like his sort of place,' Clara said. The house was as dilapidated as all the others.

'I don't think he lives there,' the Doctor agreed. 'So what does he keep inside that he doesn't want anyone else to find?'

'Think we should find out?'

'Don't you?'

'Absolutely,' Clara said. 'So, do we wait for him to leave? Or confront him now?'

'Oh I always favour the direct approach. Come on.'

The Doctor set off at a brisk pace for the house, Clara hurrying to keep up. The door was closed and locked, but a quick application of the sonic screwdriver soon saw them inside. The narrow hallway was unfurnished. Wallpaper peeled from the cracked plaster and the floor was bare boards.

There were two reception rooms and a rather

primitive kitchen on the ground floor. The two upper storeys boasted a bathroom and three bedrooms. All were empty.

'Where did he go?' Clara hissed.

'I don't know,' the Doctor said. 'But there's obviously no need to whisper.'

A back door from the small kitchen gave out into a yard. A gate from there opened into a narrow alley that led back to the street. They returned to the house and checked the rooms again. But all were empty and unfurnished.

'What was that?' the Doctor said as they stood in one of the front rooms on the ground floor.

'What?' Clara strained to hear. There was something, a faint noise like a light tapping sound. 'Something outside in the street?'

The Doctor shook his head. 'I think it's coming from the next room.'

'It's gone now,' Clara realised, following him out.

The other reception room was as empty as the first.

'Perhaps you're right,' the Doctor said.

'Always possible. It does happen.'

'Perhaps it was something outside.' The Doctor crossed to the window. The glass was dusty and one pane was cracked across. Another pane was completely missing. 'Ah,' he said quietly. 'Interesting.'

Clara joined him staring murkily into the street outside. 'Can't see anything.'

'I meant this.' The Doctor pointed downwards. A piece of paper lay on the windowsill, folded into the shape of a bird.

'More origami. That can't be a coincidence.'

'No,' the Doctor agreed. He picked up the delicate shape and examined it. 'Hasn't been here long, it's not dusty enough.' He dropped it back onto the windowsill. 'But I can't believe our Mr Milton came here just to leave a paper bird behind.'

'What do you think he's up to?' Clara said. 'Something that needs power, right? I mean an advanced form of power that could generate the spike we picked up.'

'Whatever he's up to, it's not good. A man's dead,' the Doctor told her. 'I can't believe that's not connected. Especially now,' he added, nodding at the origami bird lying close by.

'You think Milton's up to no good?'

'He's definitely up to something. I'd like to know what it is before we reveal our own credentials. The less he knows about us for the moment, the better.'

'And now what? We don't even know where he's gone.'

They walked slowly back across the room and out into the hall.

'If we work out what happened to poor Mr Hapworth, then we go a good way to working out what's really going on here,' the Doctor said.

'He was at the Carnival,' Clara said. 'And so was Milton. Another connection?'

'Could be. And then there's those birds…' The Doctor paused, tapping his finger against his chin. 'We should probably bring that one with us. It might repay a closer examination.'

'Taking a piece of folded paper into protective custody,' Clara said as she followed him back into the room. 'That's a first.'

'Not yet it isn't,' the Doctor said from the window.

'How do you mean?'

'It's not here.'

Clara joined him, looking down at the dusty windowsill. Sure enough the origami bird was gone.

The Doctor held his hand up in front of the missing pane of glass. 'There a breeze. It might have blown away.'

Clara looked round. 'But where too? It's not on the floor. There's no sign of it.'

'There's a gap here between the sill and the window. Maybe it slipped down there.'

'Well if it did we're not getting it back. Is it important?'

The Doctor considered, eyebrows knitted together and forehead furrowed. 'I don't see how it could be, really. Not in itself. Someone left it here. Someone left three more at Hapworth's, according to Vastra. The question is, who? And why?'

Chapter

6

The late afternoon sun struggled weakly through the scattering of clouds. The light was already failing, and in another hour it would be twilight. The snow was crisping underfoot as the day grew chillier. The Doctor and Clara let themselves out of the front door of the empty townhouse and headed back towards the river. Had either of them turned and looked the other way down the street, they might have seen what looked like a large snowflake dancing in the air, carried by the breeze.

A closer look would have revealed that the pale shape was not a snowflake at all. It was a small piece of paper, folded into the shape of a bird. Tiny, angular wings beat rhythmically as it fluttered on its way. Not a random, chaotic route through the air. It turned at the street corner, and set off along the next street, dancing and trembling through the afternoon.

At the corner of the street, a man and woman watched the approach of the stylised bird. The man wore a dark overcoat and carried a silver-topped ebony cane. The woman was wrapped in a long, red cloak. The hood was drawn up over her head, but the pale sunshine illuminated her delicate features as she looked up at the bird. As it drew nearer, she held out her arm, the scarlet material hanging down from it like a shimmering waterfall of blood.

The paper bird alighted on the outstretched arm. Its wings continued to beat for a few moments.

'Welcome, my little friend,' Silhouette murmured. 'And what have you come to tell us?'

The bird's wings stilled. For a moment it remained upright on the red material. Then it toppled over and lay on its side. Inert. Just a piece of paper.

'May I?' Milton asked, holding out his hand.

Silhouette lifted the bird from her arm with her other hand. She slowly unfolded the wings, then the body, smoothing the creature out into a single sheet of paper which she glanced at, and then handed to Milton with a smile.

One side of the paper, the side that had been folded away from view, was covered with handwriting. Neat, feminine, but regular.

She said: 'More origami. That can't be a coincidence.'

He said: 'No. Hasn't been here long, it's not dusty enough. But I can't believe our Mr Milton came here just to leave a paper bird behind.'

She said: "What do you think he's up to? Something that needs power, right? I mean an advanced form of power that could generate the spike we picked up."

He said: "Whatever he's up to, it's not good. A man's dead. I can't believe that's not connected. Especially now."

She said: "You think Milton's up to no good?"

He said: "He's definitely up to something. I'd like to know what it is before we reveal our own credentials. The less he knows about us for the moment, the better."

She said: "And now what? We don't even know where he's gone?"

Milton nodded and smiled as he read through the text. 'Well done, Silhouette.'

'Enlightening?' she asked.

'Oh, very enlightening.'

'I told you there was something odd about those two. Odd and dangerous.'

'Your instincts as ever were correct. Affinity had similar anxieties. Well, now we know.' He glanced down at the paper in his hand. 'This Doctor is no more a Victorian gentleman than I am.' He screwed the paper into a ball suddenly and threw it away. 'We must deal with him, and with his friends.'

'But what brought them to the Carnival?' Silhouette wondered.

'"A man is dead," the Doctor said,' Milton told her. 'That must be Hapworth.'

'Do they know what he saw?'

'No, or they wouldn't be investigating the Carnival. They wouldn't need to. They would already know about you.'

'Then they are stumbling about in the dark,' Silhouette told him.

'Yes. But the danger is that they will stumble into something significant. I want them dealt with, Silhouette. Talk to Affinity. Sort it out. Quickly.'

They walked slowly back along the street. On the pavement behind them, a crumpled ball of paper lay in the snow. It trembled, perhaps in a breeze, damp soaking slowly through it. Dark ink smudged and smeared, and dripped into the white snow. Like blood from a wound.

The light was fading quickly. Clara could see the gas lamps coming on along the Embankment. Pale luminescence crept slowly along and casting a glow as far as the Frost Fair. Here lights were coming on as well, reflected back off the snow on the ground and the ice on the river to give the whole area an eerie, unreal quality.

'I thought they had lamp-lighters to go round putting the lights on,' she said.

'Not any more,' the Doctor told her. 'In the early days of gas lamps that's how it worked, but by now they're almost all automatically controlled. They're a clever lot, the Victorians. Invented all sorts of things, including powered flight.'

'No,' Clara told him. She knew this one. 'That was the Wright Brothers. The first powered flight was at Kittyhawk in America.'

'They had good publicists,' the Doctor replied. 'Everyone remembers the Wright Brothers. But that was the first powered flight *outdoors*.'

'Outdoors?'

'The Victorians had powered flight long before that, but indoors. Inside big warehouses. It was a sort of gimmick. A spectacle. An amusement. They didn't regard it as being especially useful.'

'So they let the Wright Brothers take the credit?'

'It's not the British way to boast, or to steal other people's thunder. They invented the computer during the Second World War and didn't bother to tell anyone about it for decades. I bet the kids in your class are all only too happy to let someone else take the credit when they do well at something. The same way that I'm always happy for you to take the credit for our achievements.'

She could see from the way his mouth twitched that he was joking, and punched his shoulder lightly. 'We should find Jenny. If she's still here.'

'She is.' The Doctor pointed to the slight, dark-haired young woman walking towards them.

*

With the afternoon turning to evening and the temperature dropping, Jenny suggested they all return to Paternoster Row for supper and the benefit of a warm fire. Clara was more than happy to agree. The cold was eating through the soles of her boots and she wasn't sure she had much feeling left in the tips of her fingers.

Strax appeared briefly at dinner, telling them proudly that his own investigations were ongoing and that he expected to eliminate some suspects soon. By 'eliminate', Clara did not think he meant exonerate them from suspicion. For most of the evening, she and the Doctor sat with Vastra and Jenny in the drawing room, chatting over tea and later wine.

Inevitably, their discussions returned to the dead of Marlowe Hapworth and the day's investigations.

'He was definitely at the Carnival,' Jenny said. 'I found several people as swore they'd seen him. And he was especially interested, according to one geezer I spoke to, in the shadow puppet show. Went back afterwards to find the people as run it.'

'Silhouette,' the Doctor said. 'We spoke to her too. It was an impressive show.'

'You think Hapworth might have seen something he shouldn't?' Vastra asked.

'Backstage at the Shadowplay,' Clara added.

'I think he saw, or overheard something,' the Doctor agreed. 'Not necessarily to do with the Shadowplay.

Maybe he went back into the tent and found someone else there, or heard someone talking through the tent wall. Or…' He lapsed into silence, staring into the fire.

'What about the scene of the crime?' Clara asked. 'Any good clues there?'

'Alas, no,' Vastra admitted. 'A dead body in a locked room. Simple, and quite impossible.'

'What about the origami connection?'

'The what?' Jenny asked.

Clara gave them a brief account of how they had followed Milton to the empty house, and the origami bird they had found on the windowsill.

'A connection,' the Doctor said. 'Possibly a significant one. But I still don't see how it all fits together.' He leapt to his feet. 'I know what we need!'

'What?' Clara asked.

'A good night's sleep. Followed by a hearty breakfast. Then another day of investigating.'

'But investigating what?' Vastra said. 'There is little more to be learned either from Hapworth's study or from his manservant.'

'The Carnival of Curiosities seems to be the focal point,' the Doctor said. 'Everyone goes there – Hapworth, Milton… But why? Who or what are they there to see?'

'You reckon it's worth going back again?' Jenny asked.

'I do.' The Doctor was walking back and forth,

his fingers pinching the bridge of his nose as he considered. 'I think I'll have another word with Miss Silhouette.'

'You just fancy her,' Clara said.

'Is she very pretty?' Vastra asked.

'Oh yes,' Clara said. 'On a scale of one to ten she's about a twelve.'

'Really?' Jenny asked the Doctor.

He seemed to be inspecting his fingernails. 'What? Oh, I don't know. Can't say I really noticed.'

Chapter

7

Clara woke late, and found that everyone else was already up and about. Strax had disappeared off to the East End to continue his own investigations. The Doctor and Vastra were chatting over tea and toasted crumpets. Jenny was busy somewhere in the house.

Vastra had apparently promised the police inspector in charge of the Hapworth investigation that she would apprise him of any progress. There was none, of course – and he probably wasn't interested anyway. Anything that suggested Hapworth's death was not suicide at all but an impossible murder within a locked room was likely to be met with a distinct lack of enthusiasm. The Doctor, Jenny and Clara, meanwhile, set off for the Frost Fair.

Outside, it was just as cold but for the moment at least the snow had stopped falling. The skies would have been clear except that the London smog swathed the entire city in a blanket of grey. The Palace of Westminster loomed out of the smoky air as they passed it, little more than a pencil-sketch outline. The muffled sound of Big Ben chimed the half-hour.

The Frost Fair was quieter, perhaps because of the smog or perhaps simply because it was earlier in the day.

'I'll see if I can grab a word with our friend Silhouette,' the Doctor said as they headed towards the Carnival of Curiosities. 'You find out if anyone knows anything about the mysterious Mr Milton.'

'Why don't we come with you?' Clara asked.

'I think she might be more forthcoming if it's just me. You'll only get in the way.'

'Forthcoming about what?' Jenny asked.

The Doctor shrugged. 'Anything. What Hapworth was interested in. What he might have seen.'

'You're afraid we'll cramp your style,' Clara told him.

'You will not cramp my style.'

'Only because you don't have any.' Seeing his face darken, she quickly added: 'Joke. Just joking. Really. Ha ha. Honestly, I think you're incredibly stylish.'

His expression lightened slightly. 'Methinks the lady doth protest too much,' he muttered. 'I'll see you later. And for your information, my style – my incredibly stylish style – is uncrampable.' Then he turned and strode off towards the entry gate, brandishing a shiny penny. In moments the Doctor was swallowed up by the thick, grey air.

'I hope he isn't going to pay with a penny that has next year's date on it,' Clara said. 'Again.'

'This is going to be just like yesterday was,' Jenny said. 'Same questions, different description. So what's this Milton bloke look like, then?'

Clara described him as best she could. 'Well, he's middle-aged, just about. Thin, not very tall. He's got dark hair cut quite short and it's thinning. No sign of grey yet, though.'

'Probably dyes it,' Jenny said.

'Might well. He struck me as quite vain. He's got a beard too. Like a goatee, but short, you know – close to the chin. He was wearing a dark overcoat. Oh, and he carries a black cane with a silver top.'

'Proper gent, ain't he?'

'Proper something,' Clara said. 'You want to stick together today, or split up again?'

'Probably best to split up. But not for too long. Meet you at the tea tent again when we've done the Frost Fair?'

'Sounds like a plan. I'll need a hot drink before too long. Then we can head over to the Carnival and see how the Doctor's doing chatting up the shadow puppet lady.'

The smog was beginning to thin as the morning wore on. Even so, Clara could barely see from one stall in the fair to the next. She turned from asking a particularly unhelpful woman selling knitted scarfs and shawls about Milton. A man was approaching Clara out of the smog. His face shimmered as she tried to focus on it, gradually materialising out of the grey cloud and she saw that it was Oswald, the young tutor.

'Clara!' He seemed delighted to see her. 'I had no idea you would be here today.'

'Nor did I,' she told him. 'But you're just the person I wanted to see.'

'I am?'

She threaded her arm through his and led him through the fair. 'Your employer, Mr Milton.'

'You met him yesterday.'

'And very charming he was, too. So tell me about him.'

'About Mr Milton?'

'Oh, don't worry, he's not a rival for my affections or anything like that.'

'Oh.' Oswald considered this. 'Good.'

'So?'

'So, he's a rich man. Donates to the poor, or so I believe. Endows a trust, anyway. I'm not sure what else I can tell you. Why are you interested?'

Clara ignored the question. 'So where's he get his money? Rich family?'

'No, he made it in industry, I believe. Manufacturing of some sort. I'm not really sure exactly what. I really don't know him that well, I'm afraid.'

'That's all right. Not your fault.'

'I wasn't aware that acquaintanceship was anyone's fault as such.'

'No,' Clara agreed. 'Probably not.'

'His main factory is in Alberneath Avenue, I do know that. I had to meet him there to be interviewed for the post of tutor, you see.'

'So you saw what they make there?'

'I saw a lot of machines. Oily and noisy, but much more than that I really couldn't say.'

Clara considered. 'Where's Alberneath Avenue?'

'Not that far from here, actually. Out towards the East End, but it doesn't take long in a cab.'

'Great,' she decided. 'You'd better take me there.'

'What?' He stopped walking and turned to look down into Clara's face. 'Now?'

She gave him her best smile. 'Unless you have something better to do?'

'Not better, as such. But I am supposed to be giving a lesson in a few minutes. I was taking a short cut through the Frost Fair. I suppose I could ask to postpone it,' he said.

'Would that be allowed?'

'To be honest, I don't know. It's not something I've ever asked before. Look,' Oswald suggested, 'why don't I put you in a cab to Alberneath Avenue, and then I'll follow on as soon as I can. If I can postpone the lesson all well and good. If not, well Mr Milton is probably there and could answer any questions you have. Then I can meet you as soon as my lesson finishes, in a little over an hour. How does that sound?'

Clara thought about it. Should she go alone? But finding Jenny in the smog wouldn't be easy, and goodness only knew where the Doctor had got to. If he was still with Silhouette he might not take kindly to being interrupted.

Oswald had pulled a fob watch from his waistcoat pocket and was checking the time. 'I really should be going, I'm afraid,' he said, running his hand through his dark hair.

'Then let's find a cab on the way,' Clara decided. 'And you see if you can negotiate a stay of execution on the lesson.'

The smog continued to thin as Jenny made her way round the Frost Fair. Several of the stallholders and sideshow attendants remembered her from the previous day.

'Still can't find a man, eh?' the chestnut seller remarked with a laugh. 'I can help you there if you want, know what I mean?'

'I know exactly what you mean, and I ain't interested,' she told him. 'So you seen this Milton bloke, or what?'

'Can't say as I remember seeing a gent like that. I probably would remember. Sounds like a proper toff.'

Others that Jenny had spoken to didn't even seem to remember her asking similar questions the previous day – which suggested that they weren't going to be a lot of help in recalling any details about Milton. But she kept at it, gathering the occasional snippet of information. He might have passed by here; might have made a purchase there; could have been speaking to a man – or maybe it was a woman – just over there. Possibly…

She peered into the smog as she left the candyfloss stall behind. A gust of wind cleared the air for a moment. Was that Clara, heading out of the Frost Fair and up towards the Embankment? Frowning, Jenny set off after her. The air closed in again, and she couldn't see Clara – if it was Clara.

As Jenny neared the edge of the Fair, a figure appeared suddenly from the heavy air and collided with her, sending her staggering back.

'Oh my goodness, I'm most terribly sorry.'

The man she had bumped into caught hold of Jenny's arm to steady her.

'I'm all right,' she assured him.

'Can't see any distance at all in this,' the man said, smiling.

Jenny smiled back. At least he was polite, even if he didn't look where he was going. Though he was right, it probably wasn't his fault. The young man was wearing a plain suit with an equally plain hat. Fair hair poked out from beneath it in a slightly unruly manner. He looked about the same age as Jenny, slim build with high cheekbones and pronounced eyebrows. Quite attractive, really, she thought.

'I'm sorry,' he said, 'now I'm delaying you.'

'Oh that's all right.' She couldn't see any sign of Clara now. It probably hadn't been Clara at all. 'I'm not going anywhere, really. Just sort of wandering.'

'Well, perhaps you'd like to wander with me? If it wouldn't be too much of an imposition,' he added quickly. 'My name's Stone, by the way.' He lifted his hat slightly, allowing more of his fair hair to escape before he jammed it back down on his head. 'Jim Stone. Friends call me Jimmy.'

Jenny introduced herself, and Jimmy laughed. 'My sister's called Jenny, what a coincidence.'

Jimmy was also in service, it turned out as they made their way through the Frost Fair. He worked in the kitchens of 'a posh house out in Mayfair,' he told her. 'It's my afternoon off, and I managed to get away early to have a look at the Fair before finding some lunch.'

'Shame you can't see much of it today,' Jenny told him.

The police sergeant who had promised to keep Strax up to date on the investigations was as good as his word.

'Found another one last night, they did,' he explained as the two of them sat in a quiet corner of one of the local hostelries. 'Just like the others, it was. Nothing but a dry husk.'

'And where was the victim found?' Strax demanded. 'I shall need the exact coordinates calculated from galactic zero centre.'

'Dunno about that,' the sergeant told him. 'But the poor woman was in Little Haber Street.'

'Does this Little Haber Street have strategic significance?'

The sergeant frowned. 'It's just off Alberneath Avenue, if that's any help.'

Strax considered. 'It might be.' Bellamy's body had also been found in a passageway that connected to Alberneath Avenue. 'Thank you for the information, primitive. It has been most helpful.'

'You got any idea who or what is killing these people then, Mr Strax?' the sergeant asked as Strax stood up.

'No,' Strax told him. 'But I have a comrade who tells me that once one has eliminated the impossible, whatever remains, however improbable, must also be eliminated. Good day to you.'

Chapter

8

Despite Oswald's assurances that it was not far to Alberneath Avenue, the journey seemed to take a long time. Sat in the small hansom cab, most of Clara's view of the journey consisted of the rear end of the horse and the smog above it. She felt a little uneasy, sat on the bench seat with nothing to stop her pitching forwards and out if the horse stopped suddenly. The driver was above and behind her, completely out of view. She only knew he was there from the twitch of the reins, and the occasional words of encouragement aimed at the horse.

The suspension, Clara thought, could do with some work too as they clattered over cobbles and rattled down side streets. She thought she knew central London quite well, but with the restricted view and the absence of many of the landmarks she could have recognised on the admittedly rather logical grounds that they hadn't been built yet, she was soon completely lost.

The cab finally came to a halt with a drawn out 'Whoa' from the driver. Oswald had insisted on paying the man in advance. Clara did have some money the Doctor had given her, but she was glad to be spared having to worry about sorting through unfamiliar currency.

'Alberneath Avenue,' the driver said, touching his hat as Clara clambered down.

They were at the end of a long street. There was no need to ask where Milton's factory was. Even in the smog, Clara could see that while there were terraced houses down one side of the street, there was only one building on the other. It was a huge, monolithic, unforgiving brick façade. What windows there were seemed blank and opaque.

'Where's the best place to find another cab?' she asked, just in case Oswald failed to join her.

'Best to try down there.' The cabbie pointed back the way they had come. 'Turn left at the end and that'll bring you to Motherton Street. You should get a cab there.'

'Thanks.'

'Not that way, though,' the cabbie warned, pointing down past the factory. 'You won't find nothing good down there, miss. Mind how you go now.'

As if to emphasise the point, the driver turned his cab in the road and headed back the way they had come. Clara could hear the wheels rolling over the cobbles long after the cab was swallowed up by the smog.

Clara had thought – as much as she had thought about it at all – that there would be somewhere to wait for Oswald. A bench perhaps. Maybe even a small tearoom or coffee shop. But there was nothing. Just the faceless factory, the houses opposite – which all seemed to be empty and about to fall down now she looked at them more closely – and nothing else. Nothing except the smog.

She walked slowly down the street. There was no sign of anyone else. Also, surprisingly, there was no sound from the factory. Surely she should be able to hear equipment, machinery, people? Or was it so solidly built that no sound escaped. There were windows – high in the walls, and dark. No light inside, unless they were shuttered… Was she even in the right place, Clara wondered? The cab driver had seemed friendly and helpful enough, and he had to know his way round London.

Clara made her way back to where the cab had dropped her at the end of the street. Sure enough there was a sign attached to the end of the factory: 'Alberneath Avenue' it said in faded lettering. This was the right place. But there was no sign of life, and no sign of any way in to the factory either. The entrance must be on another street. Maybe that was why it was so quiet – this part of the factory simply wasn't in use.

In which case, it made sense to walk round the building and see what she could find – people, activity, a way in… It made sense, another part of Clara's mind told her as she set off down a narrow side alley, to wait for Oswald. But he could be ages yet. She didn't know how long it would take him to excuse himself from his tutorial duties. Or if he couldn't, then how long would he be? Better if she'd cased the joint already and at least found the way in.

The alley was dark and claustrophobic, the smog making it seem even narrower and the walls either side closing in oppressively. Clara hurried along, her heels echoing on the cobbles. A darker patch of the wall resolved itself into an opening. Heavy wooden doors set back into the wall must lead inside. Clara tried them, but they barely moved – locked or bolted firmly. She gave them a frustrated kick and moved on.

Maybe the whole place was shut down. She didn't know how long ago Oswald had been here. Perhaps Milton had closed the place since then. Even so, she thought, there might be some clue inside. Something to tell her who he really was and what he was up to.

Another alcove with more wooden doors – also locked. It was as easy to keep going as to turn back. The alley turned abruptly, still following the wall of the huge building. Soon Clara arrived at another set of doors. But these were different – larger, and flush with the brickwork. It was the closest she had so far found to a main entrance. There was a sign above the doors, but it was so faded that she couldn't make out the words.

The doors, predictably, refused to budge when Clara pushed and pulled at them. But there was a smaller door set into one of the large ones. Not expecting any more encouraging results, Clara tried the handle. And the door creaked open.

She stepped inside. The building was a shell. A huge, empty space. Smog had crept inside, curling through cracks in the dusty windows where light struggled to follow. Looking up, Clara could see the rafters, high above. The far wall, all but lost in shadows and the misty air, must be on Alberneath Avenue. She had walked down the other side of it. No wonder she had heard nothing.

Even as she contemplated the silence, there was a sudden fluttering, beating, high above her. A bird, probably, trapped inside. She walked slowly across the solid floor. There were the remains of fixings and holes where machinery had stood. Probably not that long ago, Clara thought. There was a smell of oil a well as dust and damp. The remains of the metal brackets gleamed in the dim light. If they'd been left for long surely they would have gone rusty – like the metal edges of the windows.

Further in, and she could make out something else on the ground. It looked like snow, but she couldn't see where it might have blown in. A scattering of white. As she approached it resolved itself into small shapes, like confetti. She crouched down as she reached the first, and picked it up. A piece of paper, folded into the shape of a small bird…

Behind her, the door slammed shut. Clara turned abruptly at the sound. The wind? She hadn't felt a breeze. With rising anxiety, she ran back to the door. It was locked. But there was no key. No keyhole. What there was, she saw, was a small plastic keypad fitted to the wall close by. The sort of security lock she might find in her own time with no surprise at all. But here, in the 1890s it was totally and frighteningly out of place.

Her fingers trembled. Something tugged at them. She held up her hand, and saw that the paper bird's wings were moving as it struggled to break free of her grasp. She let go in surprise, and the creature fluttered away, dancing up through the air like a large moth.

Behind it, the whole floor was coming to life. Pale paper shapes lifted into the air. A mass of tiny folded stylised birds rising up. Swarming. Suddenly hurtling towards her across the factory.

In moments, Clara was enveloped. A blizzard of paper beating at her. The sharp edge of a wing sliced across the back of her hand as she tried to defend herself. Tried to beat away the creatures that battered at her. She ran, but they kept pace, swirling round her head, blocking her vision. Smothering everything in a whirl of white, scratching and scraping at her.

Her foot caught on a metal bracket set in the floor and Clara crashed to the ground. Her head cracked down and she closed her eyes, knowing it would smash hard into the floor. But the impact never came. She opened her eyes and saw that she was lying with her head over the edge of a pit – a wide opening in the ground. So deep she couldn't see the bottom. Another few steps and she would have gone over the edge and fallen to her certain death.

She struggled back to her feet. Plucked a paper bird out of the air. Ripped it to pieces even as it struggled to escape. The torn paper danced away like snowflakes.

The whole world was white. Driving at Clara, forcing her back, towards the pit behind her. She was off balance, couldn't see, her face and hands scratched to pieces. She dropped to her knees. Maybe she could crawl out of here.

But the birds were everywhere, crawling over her, pecking at her face with their sharp paper beaks. Tangled in her hair. Scratching their wings against her cheeks. Clawing their way into her mouth. Scraping at her eyes.

She did the only thing she could – Clara screamed for help. Screamed and screamed.

And knew that there was no one to hear her.

Chapter

9

The Shadowplay tent was closed up. A signboard outside informed the Doctor that the next performance would be this afternoon. He could sneak inside and have a nose round, but there were probably people about. And he wasn't sure what he'd find anyway – really he wanted to talk to Silhouette. Did she remember Hapworth? Had they spoken? What had intrigued him? And where did he go after the shadow puppet show?

The Doctor walked all round the large tent. He called. He walked all round the large tent again, but in the opposite direction. Then he went for a brisk walk round the rest of the Carnival while he decided on the best course of action.

At the other end of the Frost Fair, Jenny was still talking to Jim. She really should get back to asking about Milton, Jenny thought. But Jim was pleasant company and they seemed to have a lot in common as well as similar interests and sense of humour.

As if realising what she was thinking, Jim said: 'I should let you be on your way. I'm sorry if I've detained you.'

'Detained me?'

'Weren't you just leaving when I arrived?'

'Oh no.' Jenny smiled. 'Thought I saw a friend, that's all. I've things to do here at the fair for a while yet.'

'I'm surprised you could see anything in this,' Jim joked, though in fact the smog was clearing a little. 'But if you are here for the duration, perhaps I shall see you later.'

'Yes,' Jenny said. 'Perhaps you will.'

He touched the brim of his hat. 'Then I shall look forward to that. Good day to you.'

Jenny watched him disappear into the crowds. She should get to work, or Clara would be wondering where she'd got to.

The morning's investigations for Strax consisted of retracing the last known movements of the murder victims. He visited the areas where they had last been seen alive, and calculated the most direct route from this location to where their bodies had been found.

He visited each of the locations and traversed each of the routes, questioning anyone he met along the way. Most people seemed happy to tell him they knew nothing and had seen no one, and he only had to resort to threats of torture and extreme pain in a very few cases.

For the most part, the information he gathered was useless, and tempered with qualifications ranging from 'But I could be wrong' to 'Or was that on the Thursday?' But something that chimed with Strax's own experience was that several of the people he spoke to mentioned a dark figure dressed rather in the manner of an undertaker in the vicinity of the actual death at about the same time as the victim must have expired.

Was this man connected to the murders, Strax wondered. He himself had seen him – if it was indeed the same person. But that was a while after Bellamy had died and the body been removed. Perhaps he was merely an undertaker appearing where his work took him. His business, after all, was with the dead…

But even so, and with little else to occupy his time, Strax decided to return to the location of Bellamy's demise and his own encounter with the undertaker. He marched purposefully through the smog, his mood darkening as he reflected on his lack of progress. 'Weakling fool!' he spat as he shoved a passer-by off the pavement. A carriage veered off to one side to avoid the sprawling man, and narrowly missed a cab coming the other way. The horses whinnied in alarm. Strax walked on, oblivious.

The area where Bellamy had been found was almost deserted. The perfect place for a murder, Strax reflected, though the fact it was so quiet meant there were few suitable candidates to hand. He located the narrow passageway and walked slowly along, examining the ground as he went for any clues. Mostly, there was snow turning slowly to a grey slush that looked like the smog made solid.

He had almost reached the end of the alleyway when he heard the noise coming from within the large building on one side of the alley. Many human sounds, Strax found it hard to interpret. But the sound of fear – screaming – was one that he recognised immediately. It was not particularly in Strax's nature to go to the help of those in distress. But if there was a battle or fight in progress, then he was more than happy to get involved. From the screams, it sounded like it was quite a good one. He licked his thin, bloodless lips and searched for a point of entry.

The nearest doors were set in an alcove and locked. But they were only made of wood – a rather primitive construction. So Strax lowered his shoulder and ran at them. The doors burst open and he found himself inside a large area devoid of walls or upper floors. On the other side of the expansive space it looked as if a miniature snowstorm was attacking a small human.

As he approached, two things became clear to Strax. One was that the snow was actually paper, folded into stylised shapes. The second was that the small human appeared to be the Doctor's friend Clara.

'Retreat at once, wood-pulp scum!' Strax ordered, charging into battle. As he got closer, he saw that there was a large hole gaping in the floor. The paper-creatures had been trying to drive Clara into it, he surmised. So he put his head down and charged into the blizzard of paper, grabbing Clara and dragging her clear.

The paper creatures followed. More than a distraction, Strax found they were actually quite violent and persistent. He could feel tiny, but painful blows on the probic vent at the back of his neck. If they flew into that and clogged it up...

'Strax – is that you?' Clara said.

'You are injured,' Strax told her, though to be fair she probably knew that. Her exposed flesh was scratched and bleeding in the most honourable manner – she had clearly put up a brave fight and Strax felt a sudden rush of pride on her behalf.

'We have to get out of here,' she said.

'Retreat?' Maybe she wasn't so brave after all. 'Never!'

'You can't kill paper!' Clara insisted as she waved her hands, swatting desperately at the creatures that continued to fly at her.

'Ah, a challenge?'

'It's not a challenge, it's called common sense.'

Strax grunted, crushing a paper bird in his fist. 'Never heard of it.'

He marched back towards the door, pulling Clara with him. But the swirling paper kept pace with them.

'When I tell you, drop to the ground,' Strax told Clara.

'Why?'

'So that you don't get obliterated. Unless you are ready to die with honour?'

'Not yet,' Clara admitted. 'So when are you likely—'

'Get down!' Strax roared.

Clara dropped like a stone, landing heavily and painfully on the solid floor. Nothing happened. She looked up, to see Strax staring down at her, his features obscured by the constant attack of the paper birds.

'Good,' he said, 'That was a test. Next time we do it for real.'

Clara got to her feet, snatching at the paper flying in her face and tangled in her hair. 'Oh joy.'

'Get down!' Strax yelled again. Again, she dropped.

This time, Strax dived aside. For a moment, the swirling mass of paper was above them, confused and disoriented at the loss of its prey. A moment in which Strax hurled something small, round and metallic into the swarming birds. It exploded, a brilliant white light bursting out. Paper burst into flames, and fell smoking to the ground. The air was suddenly alive with sparks and fire. Several of the birds fluttered away, fire eating through their wings and bodies until they collapsed to the ground, blackened and charred.

'An incendiary pod,' Strax explained, lifting Clara to her feet. 'You all right, boy?'

Clara sat on the remains of a wooden crate in the corner of the factory. Strax had produced a battlefield first-aid kit, which included some antiseptic wipes. They stung but Strax assured her they would hasten the healing process as well as sterilising her cuts and scratches.

'You got anything else useful in there?' Clara asked.

'Field dressings. Self-assembly inflatable replacement limbs. Spare ammunition, of course. Emergency rations. I even have some dehydrated water,' he added proudly.

'How does that work?'

'You just add water, and…' Strax frowned. 'Hmm,' he said. 'Maybe it's not as useful as I thought.'

'Thank you, Strax.'

'For the water?'

'For being here and for saving my life. What were those things? They looked like the origami birds we found.'

'Drones,' Strax decided. 'Programmed to follow a simple instruction set and devoid of any built-in weaponry. Primitive, but effective.'

Clara smiled. It hurt. 'So why were you here, anyway? Were you looking for me? Following me?'

'I was engaged on investigation and reconnaissance. An information-gathering mission. This is the area where Mr Bellamy died.'

'Right,' Clara said slowly. 'Ah, was he the man who was murdered? Jenny said you were investigating the death of a friend.'

'There have been several deaths,' Strax told her. 'Unexplained but similar. But what brings you here?'

'Oh we were following someone from the Frost Fair. Guy called Milton – you know him?'

Strax shook his head, most of his upper body turning with it. 'A target for surveillance?'

'Yes. And he owns this place, apparently. Not that he's doing much with it.'

'Apart from setting traps. This was an ambush.'

'You think he knew I was coming?'

Strax considered. 'It may be a defence mechanism. Not targeted at an individual, but a simple blanket deterrent. This Frost Fair…'

'What of it?'

'Bellamy said he had visited such a place. The night he died. He also spoke of a Curious Carnivore.'

'The Carnival of Curiosities?'

'As I said.'

'Another coincidence,' Clara said. 'Or not.' She got to her feet. Her head was swimming but she was feeling a lot better now. Her face and hands were stinging less already. 'We should find the Doctor and tell him what's happened here. And about your friend Bellamy.'

'You sense a connection?'

'And then some. Come on.'

The dusty light from the high windows cast foreshortened shadows of Strax and Clara across the factory floor as they made their way back to the doors that Strax had smashed open.

'We'll tell the Doctor and Vastra about the keypad on the other doors too,' Clara said as they left.

'Agreed,' Strax said, following. 'What keypad?'

As they moved out of the factory, Clara's shadow hesitated on the threshold. It waited until she and Strax had gone, then moved quickly back the way it had come. Up the wall, to the window, and then through and down the side of the building – a dark silhouette against the pale light on the outer brickwork…

The shadow crept up the side of a carriage waiting at the end of Alberneath Avenue. It slipped in through the carriage window. Inside, Orestes Milton leaned forward, hands clasped over the silver top of his cane, chin resting on the hands. He watched the shadow on the seat opposite for a moment.

'Is it done?' he asked.

The shadow shook its head.

Angrily, Milton lifted his cane and jabbed it into the seat, shattering the shadow into tiny fragments of darkness that shimmered and faded to nothing. He took a deep breath, then rapped his cane twice on the roof of the carriage.

In the driver's seat, a woman wrapped in a scarlet cloak lifted the reins and encouraged the horses into motion. The hood of her cloak was pulled up over her head, so that her face was nothing but shadows.

Chapter

10

Returning from his perambulation, the Doctor was disappointed to find the Shadowplay tent still seemed to be deserted and closed up. The board outside still advised that the next performance would be in the afternoon, but failed to give a specific time. If he continued to wait for Silhouette to return, he could be here for a while.

'You'd think she'd need to do some setting up,' he said, to no one in particular. 'And surely she's got to make a living.' But maybe, he thought as he looked round to check he was unobserved, the Shadowplay was not the woman's most important or lucrative occupation. Whatever the case, she wasn't here now, and there was no one watching.

So the Doctor undid the ties that held the tent door closed, folded back the heavy cloth, and slipped inside.

It was surprisingly dark in the tent. But the fabric needed to be heavy and thick, the Doctor realised, to keep out any extraneous light. The darker it was, the better the shadow puppets would show up against the illuminated backdrop. He took his sonic screwdriver from his jacket pocket, and switched it on, navigating through the tent by its glow.

The place seemed much bigger without an audience, its edges cast into darkness. The low benches did nothing to break up the space. But the Doctor was more interested in the area behind the screen. There was a narrow space between the limelight that cast the glow and the screen itself. Sufficient for the puppeteers to stand – there had to be more than just the woman, the Doctor reasoned. At one point in the show there had been several figures, birds, the sun, clouds, and a dragon. Unless she had a few extra limbs she kept concealed beneath her cloak. It was possible, but on balance, he doubted that was the case.

Behind the lights was an opening in the tent wall. Beyond, was another area like a second smaller tent appended to the main one. This was more like it, the Doctor decided as he entered. Some light filtered through beneath the fabric of the walls, but he still needed the glow from the sonic screwdriver to see well enough.

The puppets were laid out on a long trestle table covered with a red cloth. Shapes cut from card. White against the scarlet. He was reminded of the young woman's pale face framed by the red hood of her cloak. The Doctor picked up one of the figures – an old man, complete with ragged beard. It was cleverly done. A character portrayed entirely by its outline. No detail, no texture – just the shape itself.

He was putting it carefully back with its fellows when a thought occurred to him. He picked it up again, examining the edges of the shape. Curious... He moved along the table, examining each of the puppet shapes in turn. That couldn't be right. These must be just templates, shapes from which the actual puppets were cut.

In which case, where were the puppets themselves? He looked round but there were not many places they could be. A small cupboard turned out to be home to blank card, paper, and chalk for the board outside. He lifted the edge of the cloth and peered under the table, shining the sonic screwdriver along, to reveal just the wooden boards laid on the bare ground beneath. His frown deepened. He was missing something obvious. Unless, of course, he wasn't...

Maybe she had taken the puppets with her. Or they were stored somewhere else. Except, he had walked all round the tent earlier and there was nowhere else. Plus it wasn't just the puppets. There must be thread to hang them from, and poles to elevate the threads since there was no raised area for the puppeteers to stand. And these cut-out shapes could not be the actual puppets because they were solid, with no holes to attach the threads, or any evidence of thread being fixed or glued to them.

The alternative was just too bizarre to contemplate. Because the alternative was that these were indeed the puppets, he thought as he picked up another of the figures. The alternative was that they were animated in some manner that did not involve the use of threads and poles. That they were not puppets at all, but creatures of card and paper that could somehow be imbued with a life of their own.

Bizarre and improbable, the Doctor thought. Every bit as bizarre and improbable as an origami bird that could actually fly away…

He turned to leave, and froze as he heard something from the main tent beyond. The creak of the wooden boards. Footsteps, coming this way. He could wait, brazen it out, demand explanations… But what if it wasn't Silhouette? It could be anyone. Caution might be a better option until he knew rather more about what he was getting into.

'Silhouette?' a voice called.

So, definitely not the woman. And it was a man's voice, strangely devoid of any inflection. The Doctor lifted the cloth again and crawled under the table, switching off the sonic screwdriver and returning it to his pocket. From here he had a good view of very little, made even less useful by the lack of light. But through the gloom he could make out the legs of the man as he came through to the smaller tent. Dark, nondescript trousers.

'Silhouette?' the man asked again. Then a sigh of disappointment. The legs hesitated, then turned as the man looked round.

The man could see as little as the Doctor – probably even less – in the dim light. So the Doctor risked sticking his head out from under the table. Unless the man was actually looking right at him, he'd probably see nothing.

In fact, the man was already turning to leave. He reached out and drew back the curtain of fabric over the door back into the main tent. As he stepped through, he glanced back.

In the dim light there was no way to be sure. Probably it was just a trick of the shadows and the way the man moved, the position of his head. But just for a moment, staring up at him through the gloom, it looked to the Doctor as if the man had no face.

The house where the carriage drew up was very different to the house that the Doctor and Clara had watched Milton enter the previous day. It was set back from the road, screened by a line of trees from the casual attentions of passers-by. Silhouette dropped Milton at the front door before taking the carriage round the a small stable block and coach house at the rear.

Milton let himself into the house. The lights came on automatically as soon as he was inside. Not gas lamps, but high-luminance LEDs. Milton discarded his Victorian attire and changed into a more comfortable suit made from a body-moulded synthetic material. Then he went down to what had been the drawing room. It was now his study, furnished with a pale, unpatterned carpet. Several plain sofas were arranged round a central hologram of a log fire. A short flight of steps led up to a raised area ringed with steel cords strung between brushed steel posts.

His desk was in the centre of the area. The screen standing on it showed a selection of different views of the house or the grounds surrounding it. Milton spared these only a glance before going to a side table where a plain glass decanter and glasses rested on a silver tray. He glanced up as Silhouette came in, then finished pouring his drink. 'Can I get one for you?'

'Thank you.'

She took off the red cloak and draped it over the back of one of the sofas. Beneath, she was wearing a long, fitted dress of exactly the same colour. A large, facetted, oval red crystal hung on a silver chain in the 'V' of the neckline. It caught the unreal flames of the fire as she sat down, curling her legs up beneath her.

Milton handed her a glass of pale, viscous liquid and sat on the adjacent sofa. 'So, my dear, what have we learned?'

Silhouette sipped her drink. 'They are resourceful,' she said, 'if the girl escaped.'

'This Doctor bothers me,' Milton said. 'He affects an air of ignorance and indifference. But beneath it are undercurrents of knowledge and curiosity.'

'And the others?' Silhouette asked. 'The other young woman, the so-called Great Detective, and the...' She hesitated, searching for the right word. 'The gentleman that Empath encountered?'

'I'm not sure,' Milton admitted. 'There is certainly potential there that we could exploit. What Empath saw was almost certainly an alien of some sort. Not enough information to determine the exact species, but it sounds if he has possibilities. Especially if he is as difficult to dispose of as Miss Clara Oswald. As for the others...' He considered, holding his glass up and watching the reflected holo-flames of the fire dance on its surface. 'Well, perhaps it would be simplest to kill them all.'

'Kill them?' It was a gasp, surprise and shock, that made Milton set down his glass on a small table beside the sofa and lean across to look at Silhouette.

'That worries you?'

'Yes. No...' She frowned, then shook her head, confused. 'I don't know.'

'It's all right. I think your implant power source needs recharging. We can't have self-will surfacing and attacks of conscience now, can we?' He stood up and went over to his desk, returning a moment later with a small tube-like device. 'I've checking the shielding, so we shouldn't give off another unfortunate power spike this time. Now just hold still a moment, would you?'

Milton pressed the end of the tube to the red crystal hanging from Silhouette's necklace. The crystal glowed for a short while after Milton had withdrawn the tube. Then gradually the glow faded, and Silhouette's frown faded with it.

'I really must develop a version that doesn't need an inductive power source so close to it,' Milton said as he returned the device to his desk. 'If I understood more about the workings of the human brain I could probably remove a less important piece of it and put the power source actually inside your head. But as it is…' He shrugged. 'Now where were we?' he refilled his glass and returned to the sofa.

'You were saying it might be simplest to kill them,' Silhouette said. There was no trace of confusion or regret in her voice now.

'Of course. So I was.' He sipped the drink and nodded. 'And does that bother you?'

'Not at all.'

'Good.'

'But you also said they could be useful. Perhaps we should let Affinity keep an eye on them until we can be certain which course is most advantageous to us.'

Milton swirled the viscous liquid round his glass as he considered. 'There is some merit in the suggestion,' he said at last. 'Yes, perhaps that is the best course of action, especially as they seem very capable when it comes to self-preservation. But,' he went on, 'the Doctor worries me. He could be an agent of the Shadow Proclamation who has finally tracked me down. He hasn't taken direct action yet, so he can't be certain. But he may have his suspicions.'

'Kill the Doctor?' Silhouette suggested, sipping her own drink.

'If he is an agent, that might alert them. We must tread carefully, my dear. But whatever happens, the Doctor cannot be allowed to learn the truth.'

Chapter

11

The Doctor waited until all was quiet before crawling from under the table. He dusted himself down, and made his way back through the main tent and outside.

'So that's where you been hiding, is it?' a voice said close behind him as he emerged.

He turned quickly, to find Jenny watching him, hands on her hips.

'I'm sorry, have I kept you waiting?'

'You and Clara both,' she told him. 'Haven't seen her for ages. I was beginning to think you'd both deserted me.'

The Doctor was about to answer, but over Jenny's shoulder he could see another figure approaching. It seemed she wasn't the only one to have seen him come out from the Shadowplay tent.

'You again,' Michael the Strong Man said, pushing past Jenny. 'What's your game, then, eh?' The chains tattooed across his chest moved as he flexed his muscles.

'My game?' The Doctor peered at the man's bare chest, examining the rippling tattoos. 'Aren't you cold?'

'You out to steal Miss Silhouette's secrets, are you?'

'Does she have any secrets?' the Doctor asked.

'Leave him alone,' Jenny told Michael. 'We can look round if we want.'

'Not in private places. Not when the show ain't on, you can't.'

'So where's it say that, then?' Jenny demanded. She grabbed the man's impressively muscular arm and swung him to face the noticeboard outside the tent. 'It don't say you can't have a quick shufti round anywhere on there that I can see.'

Michael hesitated. 'Well, it's just… polite.'

'Oh believe me, we don't want to be impolite,' the Doctor said quickly. He switched on a smile. 'I do apologise if I've inadvertently caused offence. It's good that you look out for Miss Silhouette's interests.'

'Yes, well, we all look out for each other here,' Michael said, apparently mollified by the Doctor's contrition. 'Always have.'

'You've known her a long time?'

'Years.'

'And has she always been so talented?' the Doctor wondered. He glanced at Jenny, warning her to keep quiet for the moment. She shrugged and folded her arms.

'She was always good with her puppets and stuff,' Michael said. 'Had a real knack for it.'

'But recently…?' the Doctor prompted, noting the man's use of the past tense.

'Recently it's become more than just a knack.'

'Go on. Is this about the secrets you mentioned?'

Michael pressed his lips tight together as he considered. 'I'd best not say anything more,' he decided.

'You've seen something, ain't you,' Jenny said. 'Something you didn't ought to have seen.'

Michael didn't reply, looking down at the ground.

'It's all right,' the Doctor said gently. 'We wouldn't ask you to betray any trust. But something's happened. A man is dead. He saw something in Silhouette's tent, and I think you know what it was. Maybe you saw it too?'

Michael looked up. 'Is Silhouette in danger?'

'Honestly?' the Doctor said. 'I don't know. But if she is, I can help her.'

Michael hesitated, apparently thinking this through. As the Doctor and Jenny waited for a response, two more people joined them.

'Hello, Clara – you're looking well,' the Doctor said, sparing her a quick glance.

'Better than I'd be looking if Strax hadn't turned up,' she said.

'I had occasion to rescue the boy from homicidal

wood-pulp assassins,' Strax explained.

Michael looked from Strax to Clara, confused. 'Boy?'

'Ah,' Strax said, stepping forward to inspect the Strong Man's physique. 'A human who is properly built for combat, I see. How many opponents have you despatched?'

'I bend metal bars mainly,' Michael said. 'And lift weights.'

Strax considered this. 'To what purpose? Do you fashion the metal bars into primitive weaponry? Drop the weights from a great height onto the heads of your enemies, crushing them like rotten eggs?'

'Not usually. Its' just, you know, a show.'

'A show,' Strax echoed.

'Like a military parade,' the Doctor said quickly. 'A demonstration of skill and applied strength.'

'Ah.' Strax nodded. 'Good. Perhaps I can also take part in one of these *shows*.'

'Can you bend metal bars?' Michael asked.

'Don't encourage him,' the Doctor warned. 'Now, you were going to tell us about Silhouette...'

Michael nodded. 'She's changed,' he said. 'So have... Well, let's just say this Carnival used to be a happy place. A family. But recently, it's just not the same. Not since, *he* came here...'

'"He"?' the Doctor prompted as Michael again hesitated.

'Look,' Michael said, 'I'll tell you what I can. So you can help – you said you'd help, right?'

'I did and I will,' the Doctor promised.

'Then we'll talk. But first I've got another show to do. I'll meet you back here in half an hour, all right?'

'All right.'

'Perhaps I should attend this show,' Strax suggested as they watched Michael make his way back through the carnival.

'Not likely,' Clara told him. 'You're coming with us to tell the Doctor about the factory.'

'What factory?' the Doctor said.

'Exactly.'

'I see. Tell me about the factory.'

'Can't we find somewhere to sit down?' Jenny asked. 'I don't know about you but I've been on me pins all day, and Clara doesn't look too clever right now either. What happened to your face?'

'It's just scratches,' Clara said. 'But if Strax hadn't turned up it would have been a lot worse.'

They found a section of wall down by the ice-covered Thames. The Doctor dusted the snow off it and spread his coat out for them to sit on. Strax insisted on standing.

'One must remain in a constant state of battle-readiness,' he explained. 'In case of attack.'

'By what?' Jenny demanded. 'Snowflakes?'

'It has been known,' Strax told her.

'I suppose,' she conceded.

Having made themselves as comfortable as they could, Clara gave a brief account of her visit to Milton's empty factory. The Doctor listened attentively, occasionally interrupting with a question before allowing Clara to continue with her story.

'Lucky Strax was there,' Jenny said as Clara reached the end of her tale.

'Not luck,' Strax insisted. 'Strategy.'

'Well, whatever it was,' the Doctor said. 'Thank you.'

'A warrior requires no thanks.'

The Doctor shrugged and inspected his fingernails. 'Oh, well, I take it back then.'

'But in this case,' Strax said, 'your gratitude is acceptable. I am pleased Miss Clara was not badly injured in the despicable attack.'

'So you accept I'm female, then,' Clara said.

Strax blinked. 'Does the rank of "miss" also apply to females?'

'It's not a rank,' Clara said. 'Or actually, maybe it is.'

'You think these paper birds are something to do with the shadow puppets?' Jenny asked.

'Huge coincidence if not,' the Doctor said. 'And we're finding too many things that could be coincidences. I'm guessing they're nothing of the sort.' He pushed himself off the wall and retrieved his coat, pulling it from underneath Clara and Jenny so that they too had to jump down. 'Maybe Michael the Strong Man can enlighten us. He must be finishing his show soon, I would think. We said we'd meet him by the Shadowplay tent, so perhaps Silhouette will be back. In which case, a few words with her wouldn't go amiss.'

As they made their way back through the crowd, Jenny caught sight of a familiar face. 'I'll catch you up,' she told the others, and made her way over to where Jim was watching a fire-eater.

'You still here, then?' she asked.

He grinned. 'There's so much to see and do. I'm off to find the mermaid next. Apparently she's in that tent over there.' He nodded to the entrance to the exhibition.

'Yeah, well, don't hold your breath,' Jenny warned him.

'I'm not expecting too much,' he assured her. 'You want to come along? Or are you with someone?'

'Just my friends. We have to go and talk to the Strong Man.'

'Hoping to get a few tips?'

'Hoping to get some information. I'll maybe see you later.'

Jim nodded. 'I'll look forward to that.'

Jenny caught up with the others outside the Shadowplay tent. There was no sign of Michael yet.

'He's probably still juggling weights or lifting boulders,' Clara said.

'Both worthy occupations,' Strax assured her.

'He performs near the gate, doesn't he?' the Doctor said.

'Yeah,' Jenny said. 'I've seen him there a couple of times. He has a small tent close to the fortune teller where he gets ready and keeps his stuff.'

'May as well go and find him then,' Clara said. 'If he's finished, we'll meet on the way.'

'Just what I was thinking,' the Doctor agreed.

'Great minds think alike,' Clara told him.

He shook his head. 'I don't think so. It was probably just another coincidence.'

There was someone waiting inside the tent. Michael almost didn't see the figure standing in the shadows at the back as he put down his weights and turned to leave. Just a hint of movement caught his attention.

'Silhouette?'

She stepped forward, the red cloak spilling over her shoulders and touching the ground so that she seemed to glide. Everything about her was calm, serene, elegant.

'Are you leaving so soon?' she said.

Michael shifted nervously. 'I have to see someone,' he mumbled.

'I know.' She tilted her head to one side, black

hair pooling like a shadow over the red cloak. 'Oh, Michael,' she said sadly. 'I thought I could trust you. I thought we had an arrangement.'

'But he can help us,' Michael protested, her voice strung out with nerves. 'He can help *you*.'

'I don't need help.'

'You're not the same,' Michael said. 'Not since… Not for a while. Talk to this Doctor, Silhouette. At least hear him out.' He coughed, finding it suddenly difficult to speak. His chest was tightening.

'I'm sorry Michael,' she said quietly. 'But we can't have you telling anyone our little secrets, can we? I thought we agreed that.'

'No, Silhouette – please!'

His voice was barely more than a gasp. What was happening? It was like someone was tightening a vice around him. He looked down, and his gasps became more frantic. The chains tattooed across Michael's chest were moving. Not with his body, not as his muscles expanded and contracted or as he breathed. They were sliding over his skin, knotted together, twisting. Tightening. Forcing the breath from his lungs.

'Silhouette!' The plea was barely recognisable as a word.

She shook her head and sighed. Then she pulled the hood up, before stepping over the body that lay silent and still on the ground.

Chapter

12

There was no sign of Michael as they made their way through the Carnival. It was getting busier as the day wore on. The smog had cleared somewhat, and the snow was holding off, but it was still cold. The air was clammy and damp against Clara's face. At least her cuts and scratches were no longer stinging. Whatever Strax had found in his first-aid kit to clean them seemed to have helped them heal as well.

They reached the performance area close to Michael's tent to find that he had finished his show. There was no sign of the Strong Man.

'Probably packing away,' Jenny said.

'Proper storage of equipment and munitions is essential,' Strax agreed.

'I'll see.' The Doctor strode over to the tent and pushed open the flap of a door. 'Michael? Are you…?' His voice tailed off. He stepped back out, letting the tent flap fall back into place.

'No one home?' Clara asked.

'Oh he's in there all right,' the Doctor said. 'Strax, you come with me.'

'What about us?' Jenny said.

'You'd best wait out here. Small tent. Don't want it getting too crowded.'

'So what don't you want us to see?' Clara demanded, pushing past. She pulled open the flap and went into the tent. A few moments later she wished she hadn't.

The others filed in behind her. The Doctor sighed, pushed past Clara, and knelt down to examine the body. 'Well, he's dead.'

'But was it an honourable death?' Strax said. 'Did he face his enemy? Did he inflict terrible wounds and injuries on them before succumbing to superior numbers or firepower?'

'If I didn't know better, I'd say he'd suffered a heart attack.'

'But you do know better?' Clara said.

'It would be a very convenient heart attack.' The Doctor pointed to Michael's chest. 'And you can just see where the bruising is beginning to come out. Inflicted before death, I'd say. Not that I'm an expert.'

'So if it wasn't a heart attack, what happened to him?' Jenny asked.

The Doctor was carefully feeling the upper torso. 'Several ribs are cracked. This one's broken... And another.' He dusted his hands together and stood up. 'It's like he's been crushed.'

'But what by?' Clara said. 'He can't have dropped a weight on himself, can he?'

'It would still be here if he had. And the bruising would be in one spot, the point of impact, not right across the upper body.'

'Then what?'

'Death is death,' Strax said. 'You overcomplicate things.'

'Overcomplicate?' Clara said, irritated by his casual attitude. 'This man was killed. Murdered.'

'And it is too late to come to his aid now,' Strax pointed out. 'Better to determine his murderer's strategy and lay our own plans.' His tongue licked out briefly over his thin lips. 'Shall I fetch the fragmentation grenades?'

'That won't be necessary,' the Doctor told him. 'But you're right. The question isn't so much how was he killed as *why* was he killed?'

'To stop him speaking to us,' Jenny said. 'Don't take a genius to work that out.'

'But what was he going to tell us?' Clara wondered.

'Something about the shadow puppet show, about the people here,' Jenny said.

'So what now?' Clara asked.

'Now,' the Doctor said, 'we shall have to rely on my other informant here at the Carnival.'

Refusing to be drawn further, the Doctor led them

out of the tent and across to the exhibition of Never-Creatures. Clara thought it seemed rather callous just to leave Michael's body in the tent. But the Doctor insisted he didn't have time for awkward questions, and whoever found it next would see that it was reported. Any medical examination was likely to conclude that the poor man had suffered a heart attack.

'So, you having second thoughts about the mermaid skin, then?' Clara asked as they entered the large tent. 'Decided it might be real after all?'

'Oh, I think they have something far more interesting on display here now,' he told her, leading the way past the various exhibits towards the back of the tent.

'What is the purpose of these trophies?' Strax asked. 'Are they vanquished foes displayed as a triumphant assertion of power?'

'They're just exhibits,' Jenny told him.

There was a small crowd gathered at the end of the exhibition. People were standing expectantly in front of a curtain that had been drawn across the end of the tent.

'You'll enjoy this,' the Doctor told them all as they joined the back of the group.

Strax shoved several people out of the way so he could see. Clara stood beside Strax so she could see too.

There was a man standing in front of the curtain. He wore a rather battered suit and a grey bowler hat, and his patter was evidently holding the crowd enthralled. There was something vaguely familiar about him, Clara thought. The way he moved, the way he spoke… She had probably seen him introducing other attractions or acts at the Carnival, she decided.

'… yes, ladies and gents, behind this curtain lurks a unique specimen. Not a dead exhibit like what we have on the tables and in the cases around you, oh no. You may have been to other fairs and carnivals, you may have seen bearded ladies and twopenny freak shows. But the Carnival of Curiosities is the only place in London, in Britain, in the world, that can boast a specimen such as this.'

'What is it?' Clara hissed at the Doctor. 'An alien?'

He shook his head. 'Oh no, a native of this planet, I assure you.'

'Then what?'

He put his finger to his lips and nodded at the showman as he continued with his introduction.

'And so, ladies and gents, without further ado, I shall reveal to you this unique find. You are among the first, the *only* people, ever to clap eyes upon such a sight.'

With a flourish, he drew back the curtain. The crowd gasped. But in fact, Clara thought, there was little to see. A lone figure sitting on a wooden chair at the back of the tent. A figure wearing a plain, dark dress and simple hat, with a black veil pulled down over her face. The woman stood up, and stepped into the light. Her hand went to her veil.

'I give you,' the showman announced, 'the legendary Lizard Woman!'

The woman lifted the veil to reveal the green, scaly face beneath. There was a collective intake of breath, followed by applause.

Clara and Jenny looked at each other in total surprise.

'Madame Vastra?' Jenny breathed.

Jenny insisted on staying to make sure that Vastra was all right, and to pass on what they had learned so far. The Doctor, Clara and Strax took a cab back to Alberneath Avenue.

'There's nothing more we can do at the Carnival for the moment,' the Doctor explained on the way. 'Vastra can get far more from talking to the other Carnival people than we can by hanging around.'

'Not least because someone's on to us,' Clara pointed out. 'They know we're asking questions, that's why Michael was killed.'

'And why you were ambushed at the factory,' Strax added. 'Do we have time to stop at Paternoster Row and collect heavy weapons?'

'No,' the Doctor told him.

Even without his heavy weapons, Strax insisted on leading the way down the alley and through the shattered doorway into the factory. The Doctor spent a moment examining the electronic keypad on the other door. He used the sonic screwdriver to open the casing, and examined the spaghetti mess of wires that spilled out from inside.

'Remote access control. That's how they locked you in.' He jammed the cover back into place, giving it a thump to make it stay put. 'So where are these homicidal origami birds, then?'

'Vaporised,' Strax said proudly. 'Obliterated.'

All that remained was a charred black powder scattered across the floor. But the Doctor seemed more interested in the brackets attached to the floor.

'The metal's not corroded or rusty on the inside edges,' he said. 'And there's oil. Marks in the dust – I mean, apart from the ones you obviously made blundering about.'

'Thanks,' Clara said. 'So whatever was fixed down here was moved recently?'

'Seems likely.' He stood up and paced out the shape of one of the areas surrounded by brackets. 'Big stuff. Not easily moved. So, we're looking for—'

'An anti-gravitational lifting apparatus,' Strax said.

'Unlikely I think,' the Doctor told him.

'Then robotic maintenance loaders.'

'Also unlikely.'

'So what are we looking for?' Clara asked before Strax could make another suggestion.

'People. Someone must have helped Milton move the equipment, and they will know where it went.'

'So we ask around,' Clara suggested. 'See if anyone in the area knows anything. If there is anyone in the area,' she added, remembering how deserted it had seemed.

'Excellent.' Strax announced, thumping his fist into the palm of his other hand. 'Interrogation!'

The curtained-off area at the back of the exhibition tent was available to Vastra for private time alone. With her heavy veil, and disguised in a dark cloak with a change of hat, she could move around the Carnival without being recognised. She had already spoken to several of the stallholders, and of course to Jenny. But for the moment, all that any of the Carnival workers wanted to talk about was the sudden and unexpected death of Michael Smith, the Strong Man.

Vastra returned to the private area of the Never-Creatures exhibition tent to think through her next move. It was interesting, and rather gratifying, that everyone who worked here seemed to have accepted her for what she was. No questions, no lingering stares, no jibes. Alfie, the man who introduced her to the public and drew back the curtain, treated Vastra with the same polite deference as he seemed to display to all the other acts and exhibits he introduced. She was not yet sure of how the Carnival was organised and managed, but if anyone was in charge it was him. Alfie seemed to have a natural way with people, getting on with everyone.

The people who came to see her unveiled were rather different. They made no effort to hide their curiosity and fascination. But that was, Vastra supposed, rather the point. And many of them would assume that she was wearing make-up or a mask...

She was alone, with a while before the next 'unveiling' when she had a visitor. The curtain twitched, and a voice called:

'Excuse me?'

A sibilant, hesitant voice.

'What is it?' Vastra replied. Perhaps it was someone who had heard she was after information. She pulled down her veil. 'You may come through if you wish.'

The figure that pulled aside the curtain and stepped through was slight of build, about the same height as Vastra. From his voice, and his attire as well as the way he moved, she assumed it was a man. But as he politely removed his top hat, she saw that his face was covered by a mask. It looked as though it was made of soft, dark leather. There were holes for the eyes, a narrow slit for the mouth.

'Can I help you?' Vastra asked.

'Forgive me,' the masked man replied. 'But just

knowing that you are here – that you even *exist* – is a great help to me.'

'In what way?'

'I'm sorry. Let me introduce myself. My name is Festin. And I believe that *I* can help *you*.'

'Really?'

'You are interested, I think from the questions you and your friends have been asking, in a man named Orestes Milton. Is that not so?'

Vastra nodded warily. 'What of him?'

'I too share your interest in this man. I have been observing him for some time now. I know what he is doing. I know where he is. And your friend the Doctor is right, he is dangerous and must be stopped. Come with me, and I can show you.' He turned, looking nervously over his shoulder. 'But it must be now. The Strong Man is already dead, and we shall be next if we don't act.'

Vastra leaned forward. 'And why should I trust you?'

There was a sigh from behind the mask. 'Because of this.' He reached up and slowly unfastened a catch at the back of the mask, easing it away from his face with a black-gloved hand.

Vastra gasped, her hand going to her mouth, and meeting the veil that obscured her own features. Fumbling, she lifted the veil, to be sure she was actually seeing clearly.

It was like looking into a mirror.

The deep-set eyes of another human-lizard stared back at her from a face of green scales. High ridges swept back from the lizard-man's forehead. A long thin tongue licked out as he looked back at her.

'I thought I was the only one,' he breathed.

Chapter

13

Strax knew the area quite well, as he had already made enquiries about Bellamy's death. The tavern where he and Bellamy had met on the unfortunate man's final night was actually not very far from the abandoned factory. It seemed as good a place to start their investigations as any. Not having had any lunch, Clara wondered if the pub did food. But once she saw the place she decided that if it did she wouldn't want to eat it.

Like the area round it, the tavern was run-down. The paint on the sign outside was peeling. The brickwork was pitted and in severe need of repointing. Inside it was smoky, grubby, noisy and busy. A group of men in dusty work clothes, builders perhaps, was just leaving and the Doctor gestured for Clara to take a seat before anyone else got to the table they had just vacated.

Strax forced his way through to the bar – where he was obviously recognised. He returned a few moments later with three pints of ale.

'Beer?' Clara said. 'I was hoping for a G and T.'

'You don't have to drink it,' the Doctor told Clara. 'Just look like you belong here. Try to fit in.'

'Right,' she said. 'I'll just go and splash in a few puddles, soak my clothes in gin, and knock out several of my front teeth, then, shall I?'

'If you think it will help,' the Doctor told her.

'I can assist you with the teeth,' Strax offered.

'No – thank you,' Clara told him quickly. She sipped at the beer, and found it wasn't as bad as she'd expected. 'So what's the plan?'

'We should take hostages,' Strax said. 'Force these people to talk under threat of execution.'

'For the moment, we watch,' the Doctor told them.

'Watch for what?' Clara asked.

'We'll see.'

The Doctor took a swig of his beer. He smacked his lips, leaned back in his chair with his hands behind his head and looked round the bar with interest. He seemed content to sit watching for the duration, so Clara risked another sip of beer. Strax was shifting impatiently on the other side of the table. He had downed his pint in a single swallow. Before long, Clara thought, he'd be grabbing random drinkers and demanding information in return for allowing them to keep their kneecaps and other important anatomical attachments.

'Him,' the Doctor announced suddenly, sitting upright and pointing across the bar.

Clara followed his finger to see a thin, elderly man with pinched features sitting alone at a small table on the other side of the room, holding a pewter tankard.

'What about him?' she asked.

'He has his own tankard, so he's a regular. They probably keep it behind the bar. He's on his own, happy in in his own company. And he's watching. He knows everyone – see how he nods as people pass. Says hello, and exchanges a few pleasantries. Everyone likes him, and he knows everyone's business. So he's the one.'

'The one what?' Strax said. 'The one to be taken outside and ruthlessly interrogated?'

'No,' the Doctor said. 'The one we need to buy a drink.'

Once again, Strax was despatched to the bar. The Doctor and Clara made their way over to the thin man's table.

'Mind if we join you?' the Doctor asked.

The man shrugged and gestured to the chairs on the other side of the table. 'You get bored over there, did you?'

'You saw us?' Clara said.

'You see everyone, don't you,' the Doctor said. 'Which is why we wanted a quick word.'

'Oh yes?'

'Our friend is getting you a drink,' the Doctor added.

The man smiled. 'Then I'll be more than happy to speak to you.'

The Doctor's instincts had, not surprisingly, proved correct. The man's name was Anderson, and he seemed to know everything about everyone in the area.

'Rum character that Milton,' he told them. 'Turned up a few months ago and bought the old factory on Alberneath Avenue. Put in all sorts of weird machinery. Then, a couple of weeks ago, he strips it all out again.'

'What did they make there?' Clara asked.

'That I don't know. Strange thing is, I've not met a soul who worked there.'

'Automated assembly,' Strax said.

The Doctor nodded. 'Very likely. So what happened to this weird machinery?'

'Shipped out. Loaded into carts and taken away.'

'Do you know where it went?' the Doctor asked.

Anderson considered as he gulped down his beer. 'No,' he decided, putting down his empty tankard. 'But I know someone who might.' He picked up the tankard and made a point of examining it.

'Strax,' the Doctor prompted.

Strax removed the tankard from Anderson. 'Same again?'

'Oh that's very kind, thank you. Yes,' he went on as Strax headed towards the bar, 'you want to talk to young Billie Matherson.'

'We do?' Clara said.

'You do. Because one of the carts was his. So, as he was driving it, he'll know where the machinery was taken.'

'And you know where we can find young Billie Matherson, I assume?' the Doctor said.

'Today I believe he has a commission to take flour from the mill on Waverly Street to a warehouse down at Harriman's Wharf.'

As soon as Strax was back, the Doctor thanked Anderson and they excused themselves. Anderson lifted his tankard and watched them make their way to the door.

The man sitting at the next table watched too. He had followed the Doctor, Clara and Strax into the pub. Now he followed them out again. Anderson watched him go – it wasn't someone he'd seen here before. Strange-looking chap, he thought. From the way the man was dressed, all in black and with the hat he was probably an undertaker.

They watched the house from across the street. It was set back from the road, behind a high wall, but from their vantage point, Vastra and Festin could see the front door. There was no sign of life – no one came or went. The curtains were drawn across the windows.

'We should find the Doctor,' Vastra said.

'Your friend? You really think he can help?'

'If anyone can help, the Doctor can.'

'We don't have much to tell him,' Festin pointed out.

'He likes to find things out for himself.'

'Even so. There is a way in round the back. A point where the wall has collapsed where a tree came down in the storms last month. Perhaps we should take a quick look round before involving your friend.'

'It would be useful to have more information,' Vastra admitted. 'Just knowing if the house is indeed occupied, if Milton is at home, would be of help.'

Festin led the way along the road and then down a side street. They made a strange couple – a woman in a long black dress, her face heavily veiled, and the man in a dark suit with a stylised mask over his face. Fortunately the streets were quiet and there was no one to see them as they turned into a narrow alleyway behind the houses on the main street.

As Festin had described, there was a point where the wall had collapsed. Bricks and shattered mortar spilled onto the path and into the garden. The area was screened by trees, so no one could see from the house as they clambered over the wall. Festin went first, reaching back to help Vastra negotiate the rubble.

Keeping within the wooded area, they managed to get quite close to the back of the house. The windows here were also curtained, but they waited for several minutes – watching for any sign of movement. Finally, they agreed that they should risk running to the back door.

'If there is anyone there,' Vastra said, 'we should have a story ready.'

'We are lizard creatures cut off from our own people and seeking help and shelter,' Festin suggested. Vastra could hear the amusement in his voice. 'Or we could simply run away again.'

They ran from the trees to the back door of the house. Vastra had expected it to be locked, but it opened easily when she turned the handle. They found themselves in a narrow hallway. The hallway led through to an open area. Lights switched on as they entered – too bright to be gas lamps.

'Milton possesses all manner of advanced mechanisms and devices,' Festin said quietly.

'So it would seem,' Vastra agreed. She gestured to the nearest door. 'Let us see what is in here.'

'Or what about this one?' Festin said. 'It's open.'

The door he indicated was standing slightly ajar. Light gleamed from the other side, a gentler, more muted illumination than the stark brightness of the area where they currently stood.

'Very well,' Vastra agreed.

Beyond the door was a large room. Most of it was in shadow, the shutters drawn over the windows. The light they had seen came from a single source, a spotlight shining down on a book placed on a wooden lectern in the middle of the room.

'What is it?' Vastra wondered.

'I think we should take a look,' Festin told her.

Vastra walked quickly over to the lectern, checking for any signs of movement at the shadowy extremities of the room. But there was none.

The book was large, bound in leather, and open. The left-hand page was blank. On the right was a single word.

'Sorry,' Vastra read. 'Why would it say that?' She reached out to turn the page. As soon as her gloved hand touched the paper, more lights came on. A rings of narrow beams shining down round Vastra and the lectern.

'I think we should go now,' she said, hurrying back towards where Festin stood just inside the door.

But she couldn't get through. The light was solid, forming a ring of bars, the gaps too narrow for Vastra to squeeze between.

'A force shield,' she realised. 'A cage of light. Festin – help me.'

Festin walked across to stand just the other side of the light bars. 'It was triggered when you touched the page of the book. Clever. That's why it said "Sorry".'

'I realise that,' Vastra told him impatiently. 'There must be a controller nearby.'

'Oh, there is. A box on the wall over there,' Festin nodded towards the far wall of the room, close to the shuttered windows. His eyes were dark holes in the leather mask.

'Then you can shut off the force shield.'

'Of course.' He didn't move.

'Then do it, please.'

Festin shook his head. 'Oh, I don't think that would be a good idea.'

'You're right,' she realised. 'There will be an alarm. If it wasn't triggered by the activation of the cage, it will be when you shut it off. Very well, I shall wait here while you find the Doctor.'

In reply, Festin reached up and removed his mask to reveal the green scaly features beneath. His reptilian skin glistened in the light from the cage bars.

'Well, what are you waiting for?' Vastra asked.

'You know,' Festin said, 'I'm not sure you really appreciate the seriousness of your predicament.'

As he spoke, his features changed. The green scales shimmered and faded. The lizard-like face was replaced by a blank oval – a face that was almost human, but devoid of expression. Just eyes, mouth, a nose, ears. No hair, no texture, no expression. Vastra gasped, and took a step backwards in surprise.

'Yes,' the blank-faced man said. 'Perhaps a cage

is the best place for you.' And his voice was as expressionless as his face.

There was no sign of Vastra in the Never-Creatures exhibition. The area behind the curtain at the end of the tent was empty. Jenny waited for what seemed an age, but Vastra did not return.

'Were you hoping to see the Lizard Woman?'

Jenny turned to find Jim standing close behind her. 'You surprised me, creeping about like that.'

'Sorry. I wasn't creeping – really I wasn't. I'm surprised you're still here.'

'Yes, you and me both.'

'It might be a long wait,' he warned.

'What might?'

'The show. The Lizard Woman, though she's probably just some carnival girl in a mask. But she's gone now, whoever she is.'

'Gone? What do you mean, "gone"?'

Jim blinked, apparently surprised at Jenny's urgent tone. 'Um, well, nothing. Just that I saw her leave a while ago. I recognised her at once, because I saw the show earlier, so it was definitely her. Left with a man. Strange cove, seemed to be wearing a mask.'

Jenny was holding Jim's arm tightly. 'And this man took her away?'

'I wouldn't say that. She seemed quite happy to go.'

'Go where?'

'Well, out of the Frost Fair. I saw them heading for the Embankment, then they turned off.'

'Do you remember where?'

'I think so.'

'Good, then show me.'

If Jim was surprised to be marched out of the tent and through the Carnival, out of the Frost fair and up to the Embankment, he was good enough not to show it. He led Jenny along to a side street.

'They went this way.'

'But you don't know where they were headed?'

Jim shook his head. 'Sorry, but no I don't. Although…' He gave a short laugh. 'Well, it's probably a coincidence, but I happen to know that Orestes Milton lives just along here. Well, in the next road. You know, the industrialist.' He hesitated as he caught Jenny's expression. 'I can see that you do know who I mean.'

Jenny nodded. 'So what made you think of Milton?'

'Oh, just that I gather from talking to some of the folks at the Carnival that he's a regular visitor. The rumour is that he's intending to buy them out or something.'

'I ain't heard that,' Jenny told him.

'Well, as I say, perhaps it's just a rumour. Or maybe he wanted to make the Lizard Woman a special offer for her services.' He turned back towards the Embankment. 'I must be getting back.'

Jenny grabbed his arm and turned him round. 'Not till you've shown me where this Milton bloke lives.'

The house looked ordinary enough from outside. Big, expensive, set back from the road. The curtains seemed to be drawn and there was no sign of life.

'So now what?' Jim asked.

'We take a look inside is what.'

'We can't just break in,' Jim told her.

But Jenny was already marching up the drive. 'We won't break in,' she called back over her shoulder. 'We ring the bell and demand to see Madame Vastra.'

'Who?' Jim said. 'Oh never mind,' he muttered as they stood together at the door.

Deep inside the house a bell jangled in response to Jenny's pull on the metal chain hanging close by. They waited for a full minute, but no one answered.

'No one home,' Jim said. He reached out and tried the door handle. 'Goodness – it's open.' He pushed open the door.

'Then let's take a look inside.'

'I don't know about that – are you sure?'

Jenny was already in the hallway. Lights came on as she moved further into the house. Jim glanced back, then followed. There were several doors off the hall, and a wide flight of stairs leading to the upper storeys. While Jenny stood looking round, deciding which way to try first, Jim went past her, heading for a passageway along the side of the staircase.

'There might be someone in the servants' quarters who can help us,' he said. 'I'd feel happier talking to them than explaining myself to Mr Milton if he is at home.'

Jenny followed. It was as good a place to start as any. The passage gave into an open area, again brightly lit, though Jenny couldn't see where from. More doors led off this. One of them was slightly open, and Jim pushed it further open.

'Good Lord,' he said quietly. 'I think you should see this, Jenny.'

Jenny joined him at the door. Inside the room was dark, except for a ring of focused lights, so stark against the darkness they seemed almost solid. Within the circle, a single spotlight shone down on a figure standing beside a lectern.

'Vastra!' Jenny hurried into the room.

'Jenny? Thank goodness.' Vastra moved closer to the ring of lights. 'It's a force shield, I'm trapped inside.'

'What is this place?' Jim said. 'What's going on?'

'Never mind that, let's just get her out of there,' Jenny told him.

Vastra reached through the bars of light to take Jenny's hands. 'There's a control panel on the wall by the windows,' she said.

'Over here?' Jim replied, hurrying across the room.

'Yes, I've found it. I guess this turns off those bars of light.'

The lights cut out abruptly, and Vastra pulled Jenny into an embrace. 'Thank goodness. I thought I was trapped in here for ever.'

'I'm afraid,' said Jim, his hand still on the control panel, 'that you probably are.'

The bars of light reappeared. Now that Jenny had stepped forward, towards Vastra, she too was trapped inside their circle.

'Jim? What's going on? Did you do that? Turn them off again.'

'No, my dear,' Vastra said quietly. 'I'm sorry. You shouldn't have come. Now we're both trapped.'

Jim was walking slowly towards them. He stopped the other side of the bars, the light from the cage illuminating his face. As it faded and dissolved into an expressionless blank.

Chapter

14

Behind the blank-faced man, the door opened to allow another figure to step into the room. He was a slight man, with receding dark hair and a neatly trimmed beard.

'You've done well, Affinity,' he said, his intonation slightly nasal. 'Very well indeed.'

'You must be Mr Orestes Milton,' Vastra said.

'I suppose I must,' the man admitted. He walked up to the cage, standing just far enough away that neither Jenny nor Vastra would be able to reach him through the bars. 'I'm delighted to meet you both.'

'The feeling is not mutual,' Vastra told him.

'What do you want?' Jenny demanded.

'Oh, what do any of us want? Fame and fortune. Long life and happiness.'

'You won't get any of those if you keep us locked in here,' Jenny said.

Milton laughed. 'Oh a threat. Very good, yes, I like that. I can see you might be very useful.'

'How can we be useful to you?' Vastra asked. 'We shall do nothing to cooperate.'

'You know,' Milton said, 'our mutual friend here once told me much the same thing. And now he's happy to do whatever I tell him, aren't you?'

The blank-faced man that Milton had referred to as Affinity bowed his head. 'Of course. I exist to serve.'

'Good, because I have another task for you,' Milton told him. 'Empath has been keeping an eye on our other friends and could do with some help. Find him, would you?'

'Of course.' When he raised his head, he was Jim once more. 'Bye, Jenny.' He turned towards Vastra, and as he did his features shimmered and changed into the lizard man, Festin. 'Madame Vastra, it was a privilege and a pleasure.'

'I wish I could say the same,' she told him coldly.

Affinity's face blanked out as he raised his hand in farewell. The light from the cage bars glinted for a moment on the red crystal set in a ring on his middle finger. Then he turned and left the room.

'Who is he really?' Jenny demanded. 'What is he?'

'He was the master of ceremonies at the Carnival of Curiosities when I first met him.' Milton went over to an alcove and lifted a chair out of the shadows. He positioned it in front of the cage and sat down. 'You've probably seen him, introducing various attractions.'

'He's Alfie?' Vastra said in surprise.

'He used to be. Sometimes he still is. You will understand better, perhaps, if I tell you a little about myself.' He pulled a watch from his waistcoat pocket and inspected it. 'Yes, we have plenty of time.' He tucked it away again.

'You wish to gloat?' Vastra said.

'Dear me, no. Only those lacking in self-confidence feel the need to gloat. I'm very well adjusted and quite at ease with myself, I assure you.'

'Then why not leave us in peace?' Jenny snapped.

Milton shrugged. 'If you wish. I think that if I explain myself a little it will help you come to terms with what will happen to you. And I confess it would be pleasant to speak to people who could actually understand something of what I'm talking about. But if you'd rather die in ignorance, well, that's your choice.'

He stood up, gave a polite nod of farewell, and turned to go.

'No, wait,' Vastra said. 'We will listen.'

'I really don't wish to inconvenience you any more than has already been necessary,' Milton said.

'You wish to talk, and we have nothing better to do than listen.'

Milton sat down again. 'Very well. And of course you are hoping that the information I impart will give you some advantage. It won't, but please do go on hoping. Hope is so important in these sorts of situations, don't you think?'

'Just tell us who you are and what you're doing on this planet,' Jenny said.

'Ah, so you have realised I'm not local? That will help. I imagine your association with the Doctor has given you a rather unique perspective on the universe among your fellows.'

'The Doctor is a rather unique person,' Vastra replied.

'Well, I won't argue with that. But we'll get to the Doctor later. First allow me to apologise for the inconvenience you are suffering, but as you will realise I can't afford to be found by the authorities.'

'You're a criminal?' Jenny said.

'Oh, please. I don't subscribe to such labels. I am a businessman. An innovator. An entrepreneur. My name really is Orestes Milton, in case you were wondering. Well, it's actually Milton Orestes but the inversion seems to fit better here in London.'

'You say you are a businessman,' Vastra said. 'So what do you deal in?'

'Ah, now that's the nub of the matter. I develop and sell weapons. A perfectly honourable and legitimate venture, you might think.'

'I think it depends on the weapons,' Vastra told him.

'Which was just the point that various stellar authorities and indeed the Shadow Proclamation made in their arrest warrant. And indeed the subsequent trial ruling, or so I believe. I did not actually attend in person, you see.'

'You're on the run,' Jenny realised.

'A rather quaint, but accurate way of describing my present predicament. I was forced to leave my premises in something of a hurry without time to bring much with me. So in order to re-establish my business I have had to make use of the materials readily available on this rather backward planet.'

'Which is why you came to London,' Vastra said. 'The most advanced city in the world.'

'Advanced is a little generous, but yes.'

'And you're hiding here to avoid being arrested,' Jenny said.

'I shall shortly be reopening for business, but of necessity in a rather reduced and somewhat clandestine capacity.'

'And what are these weapons you trade in?' Vastra asked. 'The ones that are deemed illegal.'

'Oh well, you've just met one of them.'

'Jim?' Jenny said. 'He's a weapon?'

'My speciality is in developing weapons based on genetic enhancement. I take life forms, tweak the DNA and other genetic and cerebral attributes and weaponise them.'

Vastra was horrified. 'You weaponise *people*?'

Milton shrugged. 'And lizards, I'm not fussy.

Any life form that has potential. Like I said, I am a businessman as well as an innovator. So with Affinity, or Alfie as he used to be called, I have merely enhanced his natural abilities.'

'By stealing his face?' Jenny said.

'I have given him many faces. He was, as I said, the master of ceremonies, for want of a better term, at the Carnival. To say he had the gift of the gab would be an understatement. He could pack in the crowds, enthuse any audience, get money out of the most tight-fisted of pessimists. He did it by playing on the needs and desires of whoever he was with. Oh, it wasn't a conscious thing, but he had a talent for putting people at ease, for modifying his personality to suit whoever he was speaking with. I have merely enhanced that ability. And now he can become whoever the person he is with would most admire or respect or want to spend time with. Usually it's an aspect of themselves, a sort of distorted reflection.'

'But – why?' Jenny said. 'By making him anyone, you've made him *no* one.'

'That's a bit deep and philosophical for me, I'm afraid,' Milton told her. 'But think of it from my point of view. Imagine how useful Affinity can be, not just in luring you here, though that does rather prove my point. But imagine how useful he would be in tricky negotiations, or diplomacy. Not to mention the obvious applications relating to industrial and actual espionage. Think what you have yourselves already told him without the slightest qualm.'

'You make it sound very gentlemanly,' Vastra said. 'But when all is said and done, you are a murderer.'

'I protect my assets, if that's what you mean.'

'Is everything business to you?' Jenny demanded.

'Oh yes. I allow my assets to continue to practise and refine their skills at the Carnival of Curiosities. It is all good training. But there is a risk, and that risk must be eliminated whether it be a curious member of the paying public who stumbles across something they shouldn't, like the late Mr Hapworth, or one of the other carnival people who knows too much.'

'And Clara?' Jenny said. 'You tried to kill her too.'

'Possibly a mistake,' Milton admitted. 'I see now that she may be more use alive.'

'Are those paper birds things you enhanced as well?' Jenny asked.

'No. They are just paper.'

'But they attacked Clara,' Vastra said. 'And I assume they somehow killed Hapworth too.'

'They are stronger than they look,' Milton said, smiling. 'Properly animated just a few of them can lift a metal letter-opener and drive it home. But Silhouette must take the credit for that, not me.'

'And is she enhanced too?' Vastra said. 'Another weapon of yours?'

'Of course. She was such a brilliant puppeteer,

with a real talent for manipulating two-dimensional objects like the cut-out shapes in her Shadowplay. Now, with expanded and enhanced psychic abilities, she can control any nearly two-dimensional object. Paper, even shadows – she can do it for real.'

'Provided she uses her skills as you tell her,' Vastra added.

'Well, obviously. But the real prize, I have to say – the real prize will be the Doctor. Oh yes,' he went on, 'I know all about the Doctor from yourselves and from what he and his friend Clara have said.'

'The Doctor won't help you,' Jenny said, 'Not ever.'

'Even though I have the two of you as hostages? I'm sure he'll come round to the notion. The alternative really does not bear thinking about, I'm afraid. And imagine what a weapon *he* would make.'

'Not a weapon you could ever control,' Vastra said.

'It might take more than simple cerebral implants, I agree,' Milton conceded. 'Although they have proved effective enough in controlling Affinity and Silhouette, and Empath too.'

'Empath?' Vastra asked.

'Have I not mentioned Empath? How remiss of me.' Milton checked his watch again, sighed and stood up. 'Now I really must be getting on. So many things to attend to. But don't worry, you'll meet Empath soon enough.'

'So who is this Empath?' Jenny said. 'Another

carnival performer?'

'Empath is the key to everything. Empath is vital to how I shall make a fortune with the most powerful weapon ever devised.'

'What weapon?' Vastra asked.

But Milton was already turning to leave. 'Please,' he said, 'allow me to keep some secrets.' He picked up the chair and replaced it in the alcove. 'Even if those secrets do pertain to the end of the world.'

Chapter

15

There was no sign of Billie Matherson at Harriman's Wharf, though they did manage to find the warehouse where the flour he had delivered was being stored. Several dozen large hessian sacks of flour were waiting at the kerbside to be carried into the warehouse and stored away.

'We're expecting him back with another load at least. Maybe two,' the warehouse foreman told the Doctor. 'But knowing Billie, he won't be in a hurry.'

'So you've no idea how long he'll be?' the Doctor asked.

'Afraid not. You're welcome to wait. You can lend a hand shifting some of this flour.'

'Why don't I stay here,' Clara suggested, 'and you and Strax check whether he's got back to the mill on Waverly Street?'

'Leave you here in the docks,' the Doctor said, 'to help these nice strong young men shift hundred-weight sacks of flour round the place watched by passing sailors who've just arrived after months starved of female company at sea?'

Clara nodded. 'Like I said – why doesn't Strax stay here and help shift the flour and you and I can check out the mill on Waverly Street?'

Strax seemed to think this was an excellent stratagem, and they agreed that if the Doctor and Clara didn't return within an hour he should meet them back at the Carnival of Curiosities.

It seemed to take a long time to get to Waverly Street, not least because while the Doctor insisted he knew the way the route he took seemed rather convoluted and circular. Clara could have sworn they crossed the same street several times at different points.

'Isn't the shortest distance between two points a straight line?' she joked as they finally arrived at Waverly Street.

The Doctor looked at her sympathetically. 'This planet is a sphere, or very nearly, and the whole of space-time is warped. That's before we take gravitational and magnetic forces into account. There's no such thing as a straight line.'

'No such thing as a straight answer,' Clara muttered.

There was no sign of Billie Matherson at the mill either. Like the workers at the warehouse, they were expecting him back, but had no real idea when.

'You stay here in case he turns up,' the Doctor told Clara. 'I'll head back to the warehouse and see if I can spot him along the way. He's probably stopped off for a cup of tea or something.'

'How do you know you'll be following the same route as Matherson?' Clara asked.

'He'll want to be as quick as possible. I'll go in a straight line.'

'I could throttle you sometimes, you know that, don't you.'

The Doctor sniffed, unimpressed. 'Respiratory by-pass system,' he told her. 'Wouldn't do you any good. If I'm not back in an hour—'

'I know, meet you at the Carnival.'

'Right. And if Young Billie Matherson turns up here, come and find me.'

'In a straight line.'

He nodded. 'And every teashop and hostelry along it. He's probably stopped for a late lunch.'

'Lunch,' Clara said as the Doctor turned and left. 'Yes, I remember lunch.'

The air was crisp and the sun was struggling through the cloud and smog. It was as pleasant an afternoon as one could wish for in Victorian London, the Doctor thought. While he made his way back towards the docks, he kept his eye out for a goods cart being driven by young Billie Matherson, who the warehouse foreman had described as a short bald man in his fifties. Well, that was certainly 'young' by the Doctor's own standards.

He also turned his mind to thinking through what they had discovered so far, and what Milton might be up to – whoever he really was… Having evaded both Strax and Clara for a while, it was a welcome change to have some peace and quiet to think. He was definitely not in the mood to be distracted.

'Ah, young man,' a voice called out to him. An elderly gentleman was hurrying towards the Doctor, brandishing a walking stick. His white hair receded from a high forehead and spilled over the collar at the back of his neck. He was dressed in typically Victorian style in a dark jacket and checked trousers with a thin black cravat.

'What?' the Doctor demanded impatiently as the man reached him.

'I wonder if you can help me,' the man said, his voice assertive yet slightly fussy. He brought his hand up to his chin and waggled his fingers alarmingly as he spoke. 'I am rather new to this city, a stranger in a strange land, you might say. Yes, yes, you might indeed. As are you, I surmise.' He stared at the Doctor intently. 'Hmm?'

'No,' the Doctor told him.

The man blinked. 'I beg your pardon?'

'No, I can't help you.' Was that a bit rude? Probably, the Doctor decided. So he forced an unconvincing smile. 'Good day.' Then he walked briskly on.

A few minutes later, he was accosted again. A rather scruffy gentleman this time, clad in a jacket that seemed several sizes too big and to have been slept in. He was shorter than the Doctor with dark, unruly hair. The Doctor got the full benefit of the top of the man's head, which was lowered so that he could not see where he was going. As a result, he walked right into the Doctor, leaping back in surprise.

'Oh, I do beg your pardon. People really should look where they're going.' The man frowned, then smiled, dark eyebrows arching upwards. 'I know you, don't I? No,' he went on quickly, index finger pressed thoughtfully into the corner of his mouth. 'Don't tell me – I never forget a face. Though actually, no. Sorry, no – I think you're wrong. We don't know each other at all, do we? You must have mistaken me for someone else.'

He dusted the palm of his hand down the front of his jacket before holding it out politely.

The Doctor ignored it and pushed past with a loud sigh. 'We haven't met before,' he confirmed. 'And we're not about to meet now.'

'Oh. Oh well, that is a pity…' The man watched the Doctor hurry on. If the Doctor had glanced back, he might have seen the man's face – and his attire – fade and shimmer. His features slowly blanking out.

Several streets further on and it was the Doctor who bumped into a stranger rather than the other way around. To be fair, he reflected, the man had stepped out of a side street right in front of him.

'Good grief, man,' the gentleman announced. 'Is no one in this entire city capable of walking in a straight line?' The man drew himself up to his full, rather impressive height and glared at the Doctor. 'I wouldn't have thought I was exactly hard to miss.'

He was right – dressed like that in a ruffled shirt, purple velvet smoking jacket, and scarlet-lined cape. He stood with his hands on his hips regarding the Doctor from beneath an impressive bouffant of white hair.

'I didn't miss you,' the Doctor told the man shortly. 'I rather think that's the point.' He walked on quickly while the man spluttered angrily behind him.

The Doctor did his best to ignore the equally tall figure who kept pace with him along Jephson Street. He was not at all sure he wanted to be seen with someone who could believe that a battered hat jammed down over a madness of brown curls and an improbably long scarf displayed any sort of style.

As they reached the corner of the street, the man pulled a paper bag from his coat pocket and offered it to the Doctor. His eyes bulged alarmingly above tombstone teeth and asked in a sonorous tone: 'Would you care for a Worthington's Superior Peppermint? They're really rather good. Go on,' he urged, 'try one.'

'Thank you,' the Doctor acknowledged, pausing

to rummage in the bag and retrieve a sweet. He unwrapped it and popped it in his mouth. 'Yes,' he agreed, doing his best to articulate round the large mint. 'Very good. Very minty. Bye.' He quickened his pace.

Right from the start Affinity knew the Doctor would be a problem. In most cases, the best initial approach was to adopt and adapt an aspect of the personality of his target. So with Jenny, a young man in service was an obvious starting point. Madame Vastra was simple – another of her own species, just as alone and confused and struggling to hide it and to compensate.

But the way the Doctor saw himself was different from anyone else Affinity had encountered. He had no idea why, but the Doctor seemed to have multiple images of himself lodged in his mind. And, having deployed variations of those aspects of the Doctor's personality, Affinity was finding that the Doctor did not seem to like himself very much.

The Doctor barely even seemed to notice the young fair-haired man in pale coat and light striped trousers. The next aspect that Affinity employed was harder to ignore. But the Doctor turned on the large man in the garish coat, looked him up and down with an air of vague disgust, and announced:

'No. Whatever you're selling, I'm not interested.'

'Selling?' Affinity echoed. 'Selling?! I am not *selling*

anything.'

'Good,' the Doctor told him, and walked on.

By the time Clara found him, the Doctor was rather fed up with other people. The latest person to accost him was a young man in a tweed jacket and mismatched bow tie, with a flop of hair that looked as if it was about to detach itself from his head and go solo. He finally got the message that the Doctor was just not interested in striking up any sort of conversation and stepped aside as Clara walked up.

'What are you doing here?' the Doctor demanded, still irritable.

'Yeah, pleased to see you too,' she told him. 'This guy arrived at the mill and said he'd just seen Billie Matherson having a pint and pie at the Old Goose on Lanchester Street. Thought we should nip along and catch him there.'

'Good thought,' the Doctor agreed. 'Any idea…?'

'That way. I got directions.'

'Come on then.' The Doctor paused to glare at the young bow-tied man still hovering nearby, then set off briskly in the direction Clara had pointed. 'How did you catch up with me?' he wondered. 'You must have fairly sprinted along.'

'Don't sound so surprised. I can run,' she told him. 'Though actually I took a cab. Dropped me off just over there.'

Behind them, the young man with the errant hair wiped his hand over his face, blanking it out. He needed to find Empath, and tell him where Billie Matherson was to be found.

'You've just missed him,' the landlord said. 'Left in a hurry by the look of it.' He pointed over to a nearby table where a half-eaten pie sat next to a half-drunk pint of beer.

'Any idea where he went?' Clara asked.

The landlord shrugged. 'He went off with that undertaker. Leastways, I think he was an undertaker. Bad news, I expect.'

'Bad news almost certainly,' the Doctor told him.

Outside the pub, the Doctor grabbed hold of the nearest person. It happened to be a girl selling matches. She gave a yelp of surprise.

'Bald man and an undertaker,' he snapped. 'Did you see them? Where did they go?'

'Please,' Clara added over the Doctor's shoulder.

'Buy some matches?' the girl said nervously.

'Love to,' the Doctor told her. 'I'm a big fan of matches. Even the sort that burn for a bit then go out.'

'What other sort is there?' Clara wondered, but the Doctor ignored her.

'So tell us where they went, and I'll buy some matches. Promise.'

The girl nodded towards an alleyway. 'Down that

way. Behind the pub. Dunno why, there's only the back yard there.' She handed the Doctor a box of matches. 'Three farthings to you, guv.'

His eyes narrowed. 'That sounds a bit steep.'

She rattled the matches.

'But under the circumstances, let's call it half a crown.' He took the matches and handed her a large silver coin in return. 'Keep the change.'

The Doctor and Clara headed down the alleyway. It was just wide enough for a drayman's cart, leading to the back of the pub. The Doctor was ahead of Clara as they reached the double gates into the yard. One gate was standing slightly open, and he pushed through. A moment later, he was back out again.

'What?' Clara said. 'Not there?'

The Doctor put his finger to his lips. 'Not a good time,' he whispered. 'We're too late.'

He gestured for Clara to join him peering cautiously through the gap between the two gates. She could see what must be Billie Matherson, staring back at them from the other side of the yard. But he was *ancient*. His body seemed to be wasting away as she watched, the skin on his face sagging, drying, withering…

Standing in front of Matherson, his hand stretched out and holding the man's shoulder, was the undertaker the landlord had mentioned. If he was an undertaker. He was dressed entirely in black, dark silk hanging from the back of his top hat.

The Doctor pulled Clara aside as the undertaker turned. She caught just the briefest glimpse of his face – a sudden snarl of anger subsiding to a calmer, more neutral expression. Then the Doctor bundled her into the shadows at the side of the alleyway. Moments later, the dark figure stepped through the gap between the gates and set off down the alleyway.

'Matherson,' Clara gasped. 'We have to help him.'

The Doctor turned her away from the yard. 'Too late for that. We need to get after the man that killed him.'

'Shouldn't we stay here? Raise the alarm?'

'And get stuck with an awful lot of explaining to do?'

'But what happened?' Clara demanded as they hurried back along the alley.

'I'm not sure. But I have a few nasty suspicions.'

'Is he really an undertaker?'

'He deals in death, that's for certain. I've met a few rather bizarre characters this afternoon, an undertaker giving free samples is just another one to add to the collection.'

With his distinctive clothing, the man wasn't hard to follow. He seemed to be heading back towards the river.

'Perhaps he's going to the Frost Fair,' Clara suggested.

But he turned away in another direction before they reached the Embankment. Finally he arrived at a large house set back from the road in its own grounds. The gravelled driveway was lined with trees, so there was plenty of cover as the Doctor and Clara followed up to the front of the house. The undertaker opened the front door and went inside.

'Wait for him to come out again?' Clara suggested.

'Where's the fun in that?' The Doctor set off rapidly towards the front door. He had it open by the time Clara caught up with him.

'That was quick work.'

'It wasn't locked.'

Stepping cautiously into the hallway, they could hear the steady tread of footsteps from further inside the house.

'This way,' the Doctor whispered, setting off in hurried pursuit.

They caught sight of the dark figure of the undertaker entering a room off the corridor that led past the stairs. Following warily behind, the Doctor and Clara found themselves in a large library. The undertaker was heading towards the far end of the room. Darting from the door to the cover of a large leather armchair, and finally to hide behind heavy curtains pulled across a bay window, they found they had a good view of the man as he reached his destination.

'What is it?' Clara hissed.

The Doctor shrugged and shook his head. The undertaker was standing in front of a large glass sphere. It was mounted on a bracket, not unlike an ornamental globe only rather larger. Inside, dark smoke curled lazily like drifting smog. As they watched, the undertaker opened a circular hatch, like a porthole, in the side of the sphere. He leaned forward, pushing his head inside.

They could see his face, distorted by the curve of the glass and hazy through the dark mist. Again, the man's placid expression twisted into a sudden mask of fury. His mouth opened wide. A stream of black mist spewed out, the anger draining from his expression as the mist vented into the sphere.

After several moments, the stream faded. The undertaker closed his mouth and withdrew his head, quickly closing the hatch again. His face was once more serene and expressionless as he walked slowly from the room.

The Doctor and Clara were still staring intently at the swirling dark cloud within the glass sphere when the curtains were abruptly drawn back.

'How good of you both to join us,' a voice said, close to Clara's ear. 'Mr Milton has been expecting you.'

Chapter

16

Silhouette was standing beside them, holding the curtain which she had pulled aside. She had discarded her cloak, to reveal a long, scarlet dress beneath. A large crimson crystal set in silver glowed at her throat as it caught the light from the window behind.

'If you would like to come with me,' she said.

'What if we wouldn't?' Clara asked.

Silhouette smiled. 'Then I am instructed to inform you that your friends, the lizard lady and her maid, will die.'

'We'll be right behind you,' the Doctor said grimly.

Silhouette led the way out of the room and down the corridor towards the back of the house. Portraits on the walls above them stared down as they passed. A man with a white beard, darkened and stained by age seemed to follow their progress with interest.

'Is it just me,' Clara wondered, looking up at the pictures, 'or are their eyes really following us?'

The Doctor glanced up, to see the old man's eyes

move slightly to watch his progress. 'It's not just you.'

'I'm sorry,' Silhouette said. 'Force of habit, I'm afraid.' They entered a more open area and she indicated a door. 'After you.'

The room they entered was dark, except for the light from the focused beams that formed a cage round Vastra and Jenny.

'Doctor!' But Vastra's relief turned to disappointment as Silhouette followed the Doctor and Clara into the room. 'They have you too.'

'They think they have,' he assured her. 'I'll get you out of there, don't worry.'

'Milton's selling weapons,' Jenny said. 'He's an alien, and he's turning *people* into weapons.'

'Oh, hush now.'

The Doctor and Clara turned to see that Milton had entered the room behind them. 'You'll be telling him all my secrets, and then what will we talk about over tea and biscuits?'

'Let them go,' the Doctor demanded.

Milton laughed. 'Certainly not. They are far more valuable to me where they are, where death can be administered at the touch of a button or the mention of a certain control word.'

'You kill them and—' the Doctor started angrily.

'I won't have to kill them,' Milton interrupted him, 'if you do as I tell you. Now please, you've seen that I'm not bluffing, so let us go to my study and Silhouette can bring us some tea. I must say I'm looking forward to a little chat.'

'I'm not in the mood for small talk,' the Doctor told him sharply.

'Pity. You'll just have to listen to me and the young lady.'

'What if I'm not in the mood either?' Clara said.

'Then you can wait here in a cage. Or you can join us and be polite and have a biscuit.' Milton smiled. 'It's up to you.'

Clara glanced back at Vastra and Jenny. They were sitting on the floor inside the ring of glowing bars. On balance, tea seemed like a better option, but could she just abandon them?

'Go with him,' Vastra said. 'There is nothing you can do to help us here.'

'We'll be all right,' Jenny assured them.

'I'll save you a biscuit,' Clara promised. Then she followed the Doctor, Milton and Silhouette out of the room.

The atmosphere felt very strange and very wrong. Milton's study, in the middle of the large Victorian town house, felt more like a twenty-first-century office or hotel business suite with its relaxed seating area and raised work space. Milton was charming and attentive. Silhouette offered tea and smiled at Clara as if they were old friends.

The façade of friendliness unsettled her. Clara could tell that the Doctor was feeling much the same. He seemed happy to talk to Milton, smiling at the man's jokes. But then, every so often, his eyes became cold and hard as flint. Just for a second, as he assessed the man who in effect held them captive. Not for the first time, she felt there were several layers to the Doctor's emotions. Hidden below the surface layer, revealed in the briefest flickers of expression, was how he felt about things. And hidden below that – deep below that, and never revealed – was how he *really* felt.

The Doctor took a sip of tea. 'So, you're a wanted man. Dead or alive. A price on your head. Doesn't that give you any sort of clue that what you're doing is wrong?'

'Oh don't be so naive, Doctor,' Milton told him. 'There will always be war, so there will always be weapons. Someone has to make a profit. Why not me?'

'How long have you got?' the Doctor asked.

'Because it's wrong,' Clara told him. She couldn't believe they were sipping tea and talking about turning people into killing machines.

'I'm not defending the concept of war,' Milton protested. 'I'm merely ensuring that I benefit from it. As I'm sure you'd be among the first to point out, there's more than enough suffering generated by war to go round.'

'And you profit from that suffering,' Clara told him.

'Absolutely. I make money from it, and then I spend that money. Which keeps economies growing, creates jobs, ensure there is a profit in other market sectors. It's a good thing, surely?'

Feeling out of her depth, Clara glanced at the Doctor for help.

'You are exploiting *people*,' he said. 'Whatever the dubious morality of trading in other weapons, exploiting – enslaving – intelligent life forms cannot be justified.'

In answer, Milton turned towards Silhouette, who stood nearby ready to offer more tea. 'Do you feel exploited, my dear?' he asked. 'Enslaved?'

She smiled. 'Of course not.' But Clara noticed a slighter flicker in her eyes. Her hand went to the red crystal hanging round her neck.

'There's an obvious discussion to be had about free will,' the Doctor told Milton. 'But I've a feeling that means as little to you as morality.'

'For a weapon to be effective, it has to be reliable,' Milton replied. 'If you can't be sure you can deploy it, then it's no use at all. It has no value.'

'People have value. Always.'

'Good.' Milton smiled. 'So on that basis I can be sure you will do whatever I want to preserve the lives of the other people I have captive here.'

'I never said that.'

'No,' Milton agreed. He set down his tea cup on its saucer. 'And if you had, I'm afraid I wouldn't believe you. Silhouette here you know, of course. And you have also met Affinity.'

'We have?' Clara said.

'Oh yes. Now he is an interesting character. Or rather, many interesting characters. One of the things he can do is assess a personality, determine what makes someone tick. But I gather he had quite a hard time with you, Doctor.'

'I can't imagine why.'

'Neither could I,' Milton admitted. 'Which is why Silhouette gave you that particular cup.'

The Doctor frowned, inspecting his tea cup. It looked just like the others, so far as Clara could see.

'DNA and biometric sampling?' the Doctor guessed.

'Analysis of saliva, perspiration, skin cell content as well as monitoring of life signs,' Milton agreed. 'All beamed directly to my computer up there. Should have a result fairly soon, I think.'

'Or you could just have asked me who I am,' the Doctor told him.

'And trust that you were willing to tell me. And that what you told me was the truth.'

'Trust is a good thing,' Clara told him. 'You get nowhere if you don't trust people.'

Milton seemed amused. 'Is that so? Then tell me –

truthfully – has the Doctor never misled *you*, has he always answered *your* questions? Has he never lied *to you*?' His smile grew as he watched the blood drain from Clara's face. She felt suddenly cold inside. 'And you're his friend. Trust gets you nowhere, except possibly dead.'

'Well you'd know all about people getting possibly dead,' she shot back. 'What about Billie Matherson?'

'Who?'

'I think that rather makes the point,' the Doctor said quietly. 'You have no moral sensibility at all. No feeling for the people you kill – no, let me rephrase that, the people your weapons kill.' He leaned forward. 'What happened to Matherson, anyway? And all the others your undertaker friend murdered?'

'My undertaker friend?'

'The one who sucks the life out of people then gobs it into a goldfish bowl,' Clara said.

'Ah, you must mean Empath. Yes, an interesting case, I'm glad you asked about him. He is key to my latest weapon. My latest and, though I say so myself, greatest weapon.'

'I suspect we measure these things in very different ways,' the Doctor told him.

Milton ignored this, leaning back in his chair and tapping the tips of his fingers together as he spoke. 'He was a poor sad man when I found him. He worked at the Carnival too, though in a fairly menial capacity. It proved a very rich recruiting ground. But, you know, I don't even recall his name.'

'David Rutherford,' Silhouette said quietly.

There was no sign that Milton heard her. 'He was one of those people who desperately wants to fit in. It wasn't deliberate, but his behaviour modified depending on the mood of the people he was with. If they were happy, then so was he. If they were sad, then he had the woes of the world on his shoulders. He felt what they felt, saw the world through their eyes. Emotionally he was very much in the moment, malleable, *receptive*.'

'And that's a bad thing?' Clara said. 'Sounds like he was sympathetic.'

'Oh indeed. *E*mpathetic, even. And of course I enhanced that ability.'

The Doctor leaned forward. 'So he absorbs the most dominant emotion in the people he kills. Drains it out of them, and leaves them empty, dead husks.'

Milton jabbed his finger in the air triumphantly. 'You have it exactly.'

'And apart from killing people,' Clara said, 'how does that make him a weapon?'

'Because the people he's been killing, according to Strax,' the Doctor said, 'are angry. Very angry. Disaffected, downtrodden, seething with rage at the injustice of the world and their place in it.'

'This city is the richest in the world,' Milton said.

'And the poorest. Here live those who are the most fortunate, and the most unfortunate. The best satisfied with their lot, and the least happy.'

'I think Dickens said it better,' the Doctor murmured.

'So, what?' Clara said. 'This Empath guy is taking people's anger?'

'Anger, rage, fury. Yes.'

'Not only that,' the Doctor said, his tone suddenly grave. 'But you're storing it. Empath takes it, and then ejects it into that glass sphere in your library.'

'To create a cloud – a creature – of pure anger.' Milton gave a sudden laugh and jumped to his feet. 'Now *that* is a weapon.'

'*That* is contemptible,' the Doctor retorted.

But Milton was hurrying across the room, up to the raised area where his desk stood. He sat down, working at a thin tablet device and staring at the screen for a few moments. Then he nodded with satisfaction and walked slowly back to re-join them.

'Well, who would have thought it,' he said. 'I can see why Affinity was so confused.'

'He has that effect on people,' Clara said.

'A Time Lord, no less,' Milton went on. 'Not something you come across every day. In fact, not something I would expect to come across ever.'

'I doubt it will happen again,' the Doctor told him.

'And you have the audacity to lecture me about the

creation and use of weapons?' Milton said. He clicked his tongue and wagged his finger as if telling off a naughty schoolboy. 'When you are one of the race responsible for the most destructive and apocalyptic war ever fought. And here am I, a humble arms dealer trying to evade justice and make a decent living. Oh, we are in the presence of an expert here, someone who when it comes to war is in another league altogether.'

'I ended that war,' the Doctor said, his voice low and tense with emotion.

'It was the ending of it, by all accounts, which cost the most lives,' Milton countered. 'And every life, or so I am told, is of value.'

There was silence for several moments. 'I think we're past tea,' Milton said at last. 'Silhouette, my dear, perhaps you could clear away the cups? Then I suggest we adjourn to the library.'

The undertaker – Empath – was waiting for them outside Milton's study. He fell in behind as they walked back towards the library, his head down and hands behind his back as if following a cortège.

'Pure, raw anger,' Milton said proudly as they approached the glass sphere.

Clara could see now that there was a pipe leading from the back of the globe to the fireplace and up the chimney.

The Doctor had seen it too. 'You're not going to

release it?' he said, appalled.

'What use is a weapon if it's never been tested?' Milton said. 'Imagine what it could do to a city like London. An obvious choice, of course, for a demonstration as it is the greatest and largest city on this rather backward planet.'

'What will happen?' Clara asked.

'A cloud of anger, infecting everyone who breathes it in,' the Doctor said. 'What do you think?'

Milton turned to Empath. 'What do *you* think?'

'There will be riots,' he said, his voice as calm and unaffected as Milton's. 'Violence. Bloodshed. Murder. Within a few hours the whole city will be at war with itself. Within a few days there will be no one left alive.'

'But that's…' Clara struggled to think of a word powerful and damning enough. 'You can't!'

'As I said, it needs to be tested,' Milton told her. 'If I am to sell it as a viable, and very expensive, weapon then I have to be able to demonstrate that it works as advertised. Which is where you come in, of course.'

'Me?'

'Well, the Doctor, actually.' Milton stepped closer to the Doctor. 'Empath could kill you in a moment, of course. So please don't try anything stupid. I had hoped to weaponise you. In fact, I think you would make the most destructive of weapons. Let's face it, you're over halfway there already.'

'You can't begin to imagine,' the Doctor said quietly.

'But now I know who – and what – you are…' He shook his head. 'Affinity had trouble, and I think I would too. You mentioned free will, and of course my weapons are not allowed anything even approaching such a luxury.'

'Cerebral implants,' the Doctor said. 'Powered by crystal induction.'

'Oh, you noticed.'

'The crystal round Silhouette's neck?' Clara said.

'Keeps her under my control,' Milton agreed. 'Just as Empath and Affinity are controlled by the crystals in the rings they wear. Please.'

He gestured to Empath, who held out his left hand. On the middle finger was a ring set with a large red crystal, a smaller version of what Silhouette wore.

'Silhouette was rather wilful, I'm afraid. Which is why her control crystal has to be somewhat larger,' Milton said.

'And you're going to stick these crystals on us?' Clara asked.

'You, and the other two probably. I should say that some surgery is also necessary, I'm afraid.' He turned back to the Doctor. 'But not you.'

'Why not?' the Doctor asked. 'They look very fetching. Red is so my colour, you know.'

'Perhaps. But I doubt a crystal the size of this house would keep you in check. Which is a shame. As I say, you would make a brilliant and valuable – by which I mean expensive – addition to my arsenal.'

'Sorry if I'm a problem.' The Doctor switched on a smile.

Milton nodded to Empath who moved to the side of the glass sphere, his hand on the hatch.

'Oh, it's no problem,' Milton said. 'Perhaps you'd like to see what Empath is about to do?'

'I'd be fascinated,' the Doctor said, walking over to stand beside the dark figure. 'What is he about to do?'

'Before I test the anger weapon on a whole city,' Milton said. 'I should like to test it on an individual.'

As he spoke, Empath opened the hatch with one hand. With the other he grabbed the back of the Doctor's head and forced it suddenly, violently down to the opening.

Caught by surprise, the Doctor gasped and struggled. But his head was shoved inside the sphere – coughing and spluttering.

'No – stop!' Clara launched herself at the sphere, but Milton grabbed her and pulled her back.

'He won't hurt anyone,' Clara told him, pulling herself free. 'You'll never make him hurt anyone.'

'I think you're probably right.'

Milton smiled in satisfaction as Empath pulled the Doctor back, and slammed the hatch shut. The Doctor collapsed to his knees, his hand to his throat, coughing and retching. His eyes were wide and his whole body started to shake. His expression was one of pure rage.

Milton gave Clara a sudden shove in the back. She stumbled forwards, down on one knee, and found herself staring straight into the Doctor's contorted face.

'So let's see, shall we?' Milton said. 'Will he give vent to his anger by killing you? Or will he try to keep it locked up inside himself. In which case, it will tear him to pieces.'

Chapter
17

The Doctor's face was a mask of anger and rage. His lips drew back from gritted teeth and the furrows in his forehead deepened. He pitched forward onto his hands and knees, fingers clawing at the floorboards. His breath was coming in short gasps, almost sobs, as he struggled to contain the emotion.

'Not long now,' Milton said, his voice almost dripping with satisfaction.

Clara stared into the Doctor's haunted face, unable to look away. His eyes were bulging, bloodshot, staring back at her with a malevolence beyond anything she had seen him turn against even the most murderous and evil creatures. He raised his hand, his fingers curled into a claw, his whole arm shaking. He reached out towards Clara – for help? Or to scrape his nails down her face? His breathing was ragged – short, sharp, desperate intakes of air, saliva flecking his lips. The colour seemed to have drained from his face, leaving him pale as death.

'Clara!' he gasped. 'Clara, I—'

'What can I do to help?' she demanded.

But he didn't seem to hear her. His eyes turned upwards, showing only the whites as he leaned back on his knees, arms suddenly spread wide.

'There's nothing you can do,' Milton said softly behind her. 'I'd say this qualifies as a success.'

She felt her concern turning to rage. But even as she turned to lunge at Milton, ready to scrape her own clawed hands down his face, she heard the Doctor laugh.

It wasn't much of a laugh. More of a tortured exhalation. 'I don't think much of your qualifications, then.'

The rasp became a cough, which became a final long exhalation. Slowly the Doctor pulled himself to his feet, grabbing Clara's arm for support. His face remained drawn and pale, but the rictus of concentration was gone.

The rage was still there in his voice, an undercurrent to his words. 'You think you can use anger as a weapon against me? I've been so angry for so long there's nothing left you or anyone else can teach me about it.'

'So it would seem,' Milton said, disappointed. 'I'm impressed. Truly.'

The Doctor eased himself away from Clara's supporting grasp, standing on his own. Defiant, if swaying slightly. He looked tired rather than angry now. The effort of resisting the effects of the cloud of emotion had clearly taken its toll.

'But what about you?' the Doctor said.

'Me? Oh, you shouldn't worry about me,' Milton told him.

'Release that cloud into London and it will permeate everything. Even this house.'

'A good point,' Milton conceded.

'So you can't release it,' Clara realised. 'Or you'll be affected too. And I'm guessing you can't resist that stuff the way the Doctor did.'

'Sadly, I'm sure you're correct,' Milton agreed. 'Which is why I shall make sure I don't inhale any part of that cloud.' He walked back towards the glass sphere. 'You will notice that aside from the hatch, the only other egress from this container is via the pipe that leads up the chimney.'

'That won't help you,' the Doctor cut in. 'That cloud will disperse through the smoggy air of London. It might take a while, but wherever you are, it will find you.'

'If you'll allow me to finish what I was saying, you will note that there is no release mechanism on the container.'

'You're not planning to release it at all?' Clara said, puzzled.

'A remote system,' the Doctor realised. 'You'll

activate it from somewhere else, somewhere safe. Airtight.'

'My ship,' Milton said. 'I have it secreted in the basement of this house. There's a launch ramp leading up through the coach house outside. Not that I am planning on going anywhere. I can monitor the effects of the cloud remotely from the ship.'

'And emerge again once the cloud has dispersed.'

'I estimate that in seventy-two hours all the anger will have been absorbed by the population of London. Who will all be dead in another twelve hours. Maximum. Including you, I think, Doctor. You might have been able to resist a small portion of the cloud, but I imagine the full dose will destroy even your remarkable ability to resist. Or if not, there will be no shortage of other people enraged enough to tear you limb from limb.'

It was the man's unshakeable calm as much as anything that got to Clara. He was standing there, talking about killing the entire population of London for some sort of product demonstration as if it had no more impact or effect than handing out leaflets at a trade show. She could feel herself getting more and more worked up.

Now, especially after what he had done to the Doctor, she was unable to contain herself any longer. She leapt at Milton, reaching for his throat. But he was quicker and stronger than he looked, grabbing her wrists and pushing Clara away. She stumbled backwards, and the Doctor caught her before she could fall.

'Dear, dear,' Milton chided. 'Don't forget I can kill your friends in moments.' He produced a small device from his jacket pocket. 'I can change the size of the force cage that contains them, bringing the bars closer and closer together until...' He shook his head in mock sadness. 'Not a very nice way to go.'

'We'll stop you, Milton,' the Doctor said. 'I can't let this happen. You know that.'

'I do,' Milton agreed. 'Which is why, regrettably, you have to die. I did hope you might be useful in some small way, but evidently not. Now, if you will excuse me I have the final preparations to make for the release of my weapon. So I shall leave you in Empath's more than capable hands.'

Milton turned to go. The Doctor made to follow, but Empath stepped in front of him.

'I need my anger back from you, Doctor,' Milton said from the doorway. 'And while he's at it, Empath may as well take the girl's anger too. She's demonstrated quite admirably that she has rather a lot of it seething away inside. Regrettably, the process will kill you both.' He turned to go, then hesitated. 'I'm sorry – actually that's not true. As I have impressed upon Silhouette, you should never apologise unless you don't actually mean it. And I feel no regret whatsoever. Goodbye to you both. It's been a fascinating and stimulating afternoon.'

'I wish I could say the same,' the Doctor told him. But Milton had already gone, pulling the door closed behind him.

'So what do we do now?' Clara said.

'You die,' Empath told her.

'No, Empath – think about this,' the Doctor said quickly. 'That cloud of Anger will kill everyone in London. You must have friends out there, people you care about. Maybe you can resist it, maybe not. But think about the rest of the city.'

Empath stepped towards them, his mouth yawning open, ready to inhale their emotions, their anger.

'What if we break this sphere?' Clara said desperately.

'No good – that will just release the cloud.' The Doctor took a step towards Empath. 'All right,' he said. 'All right, you're going to kill us. But kill me first.'

'No – Doctor!' Clara called out. She ran forward, intending to push the Doctor aside. Maybe he could escape while Empath was killing her – draining her of every emotion that made her who she was. If anyone could stop Milton it was the Doctor, and she had to give him the chance to try.

But Empath was already drawing the anger out of the Doctor. She could see a dark mist, like a thinner version of the cloud within the sphere, drifting out of the Doctor's mouth and nostrils. Then it seemed to emanate from his whole body. Empath was breathing it in, his mouth impossibly wide.

'You want my anger,' the Doctor gasped. 'You want it – then have it!'

He threw back his arms and opened his own mouth. The mist thickened suddenly into a dense black fog that crashed over Empath like a huge wave. There was a scream, a drawn-out cry of pain and surprise. It took Clara a moment to realise that it wasn't coming from the Doctor, but from the heart of the black fog that engulfed Empath.

Slowly it cleared, to reveal the dark-clad figure lying on the floor. His hat had fallen a short distance away, the dark silk curled into a question mark across the wooden boards.

'What happened?' Clara said. 'Is he dead?'

'No, but he'll be out for a bit. Overdosed on emotion. He got all the anger I absorbed from that sphere, and a bit more besides. Seems it was a bit too much for him to handle.'

'So how do we stop Milton releasing this stuff?'

The Doctor was already examining the sphere. 'There's no way to disperse it safely. And I don't see a way to detach the sphere from the release mechanism.'

'Are you saying we can't stop him?'

The Doctor tapped his index finger against his chin as he considered. 'We can stop him if we get to him in time.'

'And if not?'

'Then we need a contingency plan.' He turned to look at the prone figure of Empath. 'Yes, that might work,' he murmured. Then, louder: 'Right, you find Vastra and Jenny and get them out of that cage. Then they can help you find Milton. Maybe you can stop him. Maybe not.'

'And what about you?'

'Oh, I'm going to wait here for a minute, just until our friend starts to recover. Having absorbed all that anger, he'll be madder than hell. And he'll be maddest at me.'

'Then shouldn't you get well away from him?'

'Absolutely not.' The Doctor grinned suddenly. It was a while, Clara realised, since she'd seen him genuinely smile, so things must be looking up. Unless he'd just gone completely bonkers, she thought, as he said: 'I'm going to take him to the Carnival. He'll love it.'

'You what?'

'The Carnival of Curiosities. If you and Vastra and Jenny can't stop Milton, then that's the one place I can find what I need to stop that cloud in there from turning everyone into angry killers.'

'Right. You want to explain that.'

'Love to,' he told her. 'But there's no time – go on.'

Clara nodded. 'OK, if you know what you're doing.'

In answer the Doctor gave her a wink. Clara decided

that would have to do as far as reassurance went. She edged past Empath, who was beginning to stir, slowly pushing himself up from the floor. She hurried down the corridor towards the room where Vastra and Jenny were imprisoned.

Hearing the sound of footsteps behind her, Clara glanced back. She saw the Doctor emerge rapidly from the library and set off towards the front door. A moment later, the dark, funereal figure of Empath followed. Even from down the corridor, Clara could hear him hissing with rage.

'Oh, Doctor,' she murmured, 'I hope you do know what you're doing.'

'Oh, Doctor,' the Doctor muttered to himself as he emerged from Milton's house, 'I hope you do know what you're doing.'

The tricky thing was keeping Empath within sight but not allowing him to get too close. The Doctor wasn't at all sure he could survive another emotion-drain like the last. If he hadn't already been tanked up on additional anger it would have finished him. He was also relying on Empath being so focused on coming after *him* that the man – if you could still call him a man – would not vent his wrath on anyone else who got in his way.

The other unknown factor was just how long the Doctor had before Milton released the cloud of anger over London. He knew that Clara and the others would do their best to stop him, but realistically, it was going to happen. Milton might be charming and chatty, but he was also quite obviously ruthless, capable, and quite probably vindictive. Plus, of course, it was always best to assume and plan for the worst case. Sometimes, the Doctor was pleasantly surprised when the worst case then didn't happen. But not often.

Arriving back at the Frost Fair, the Doctor was pleased to see that it was busy. Afternoon was turning to evening and the light was drawing in, so he waited a moment to be absolutely sure that Empath saw him head down into the gathering crowds. He needed time to prepare, and time for Milton to act. It wouldn't do for Empath to find him too soon. So the crowds were a welcome camouflage, somewhere to lose himself for a while.

Several times, looking back through the mass of people, the Doctor caught sight of Empath's distinctive black hat above the crowd. He would probably guess eventually that the Doctor was making for the Carnival. It was unlikely he would guess why. Even so, the Doctor took a roundabout route, in case Empath caught sight of him.

By the time he arrived at the Carnival, there was no sign of Empath. Unable to find his ticket from earlier, the Doctor fumbled for a penny. He ought really, he reflected, to get in free of charge since he was here to save the world. A family was just leaving, mother father and a small boy whose face was a radiant smile and whose mouth had forgotten how to stop working.

'And a real mermaid as well,' he was saying. 'An actual real mermaid.'

'What was your favourite?' the mother asked as they brushed past the Doctor. He couldn't help hesitating to find out. The answer surprised him.

'The Strong Man,' the boy said. 'He was *awesome*. The way he can bend those metal bars. And lift those heavy weights. What about when he picked that man up with one hand because the man said it was all a trick and the weights weren't really heavy?'

The boy's gushing enthusiasm faded into the crowd. What it was to be young, the Doctor thought. But – the Strong Man? It seemed unlikely that poor Michael had made a miraculous recovery and returned from the dead, but then again anything – as the Doctor well knew – was possible.

There was quite a crowd gathered round the area where the Strong Man performed. The Doctor pushed his way through, gasps of astonishment and awe accompanying his progress. When he was close enough to see what was going on, he smiled along with the rest of the audience. It really was quite impressive.

The performance ended with the Strong Man

taking a thick metal bar and bending it. In fact, he more than bent it, he practically folded it in half. Then to make the point, he unfolded it and pulled it straight again. The Doctor clapped along with everyone else. The Strong Man took a bow and retreated to his small tent.

As the crowd gradually dispersed, the Doctor made his way over to the tent and went inside.

'That was an excellent performance,' he said. 'Really impressive. You know how to work an audience. Which is good, because I need you to help me gather together all the performers we can find. Jugglers, clowns, acrobats, fire-eaters, all of them.'

'You are assembling an army?' Strax asked.

'In a manner of speaking,' the Doctor agreed. 'An army of performers who are going to help us save the world, or at least the city of London.'

'We are going to fight?' Strax asked. 'Lay down covering fire and assault the enemy in a devastating full frontal attack with scissor grenades, fragmentation explosives, and heavy laser artillery?'

'Not exactly,' the Doctor admitted. 'We are going to put on a show. We're going to give the performance of our lives.'

Strax said nothing for a moment as he absorbed this information. Then he nodded, and his thin bloodless lips curved into a satisfied smile. 'Excellent.'

Chapter

18

The only light came from the door behind Clara and the solid bars of light shining down from the ceiling. Vastra and Jenny were still sitting inside the circle. They both got to their feet as Clara entered.

'Thank goodness,' Jenny breathed.

'You are alone?' Vastra said.

'Milton's pushed off somewhere and the Doctor's up to something clever,' Clara explained. 'So how do I get you out of there?'

Vastra pointed out the control panel on the wall by the window. It took Clara a few attempts to shut off the bars, but finally the cage dissolved into darkness.

'We have to stop Milton,' Clara told them. 'He's got this cloud of pure anger or something which he's planning to release into London.'

'To what effect?' Vastra asked.

'It's a weapon. It turns everyone who breathes it in or touches it into a maniac killer zombie. Or something.'

'Why's he doing this?' Jenny said.

'To demonstrate to potential buyers that it works,' Clara said.

'He is trying to re-establish his business as an arms supplier,' Vastra said. 'But he has to be careful. If the Shadow Proclamation locate him, I imagine from what he has told us that they would execute him.'

'So where is he, then?' Jenny demanded. 'Let's go and sort him out.'

Milton had mentioned his ship was concealed beneath the house. But Clara reckoned the best place to start looking for him was the study where he had given them tea. She led Vastra and Jenny back through the house. There was no sign of anyone else.

The study too appeared empty.

'There might be something useful on his desk,' Jenny suggested.

'A good thought,' Vastra agreed.

But the desk was clear, apart from a small futuristic handgun and the compact computer and its screen that Clara had seen Milton use earlier.

'Wherever he is, he's unarmed,' Jenny said. She offered the gun to Vastra. 'Madame?'

Vastra took it, examined it briefly, and put it back on the desk. 'It is keyed to his biological signature. No good to us, as only Milton can operate it. This, however, may be more use.' She passed her hand across the surface of the computer, and the screen came to life. 'Arrogant of him not to secure it.'

'He obviously doesn't expect visitors to get this far,' Clara said.

Most of what flashed across the screen meant nothing to her – symbols and equations, writing in a language she had never seen before. But then Vastra found a way into the security systems. Pictures of various areas of the house appeared in windows on the screen. One showed a view of a sleek spaceship at the end of a sloping ramp.

'That must be how he came here,' Clara said.

'And how he hopes to escape,' Vastra agreed. 'Although if the authorities are closing in on him, they'll track the engine signature as soon as he launches.'

Another window gave a view of the study, the three of them grouped round the screen. Clara glanced towards where the camera must be, but she couldn't see it. The device was well hidden. More empty rooms, most of them obviously unused. Then at last, Milton appeared on the screen. The window showed the glass sphere, the black cloud of anger swirling round inside it as Milton checked the pipe leading from it. He made an adjustment to a valve, and nodded with evident satisfaction.

'You know where this is?' Vastra asked.

'Library,' Clara told her. 'This way.'

'Can we stop him releasing that stuff?' Jenny asked

as they hurried back through the house.

'He said the release mechanism worked on a remote control,' Clara said. 'He's just checking it's all set up. I think he has to release it from somewhere else. He wanted to be on his ship and safely quarantined from it – so maybe the release control is on the ship.'

'Then we may be able to stop him after all,' Vastra said.

Milton was still working at the sphere, framed between two high-backed armchairs, as the three of them rushed into the library. He looked up as they entered. His surprise was wiped away by a smile of affable greeting.

'You're just in time,' he told them. 'If you wait just a few minutes, you'll see the tank empty and clear as I vent the cloud into the air above London.'

'You will do no such thing,' Vastra told him.

'The game's up,' Clara added. 'I've always wanted to say that, so I'll say it again – the game's up. I know you can't release it from here because you made the mistake of telling us that.'

'And you're going nowhere,' Jenny said.

Milton frowned. 'How tiresome,' he murmured, reaching into his pocket.

'If you're looking for your gun, it's on your desk,' Clara told him.

'Thank you. But actually I was looking for this.' Milton pulled a watch from his pocket, checking the time quickly and the returning it. 'I am on a schedule, I'm afraid. Several prospective buyers are watching on long-range sensors to see what happens when I release my friend here.' He patted the sphere.

'Then they'll be disappointed,' Vastra said.

Milton seemed to ignore her. 'My transmissions may have alerted the authorities to my general location. They won't have an exact fix, but I do have to be a bit careful for the next few days. Did you know,' he went on, as if recounting a particularly amusing anecdote, 'that the Shadow Proclamation arranged to have me tried *in absentia*? Apparently, I'm to be executed on sight. So you'll forgive me if I leave you to indulge your fantasies while I press on with more important matters.'

'You ain't going nowhere,' Jenny told him. She flexed her hands and adopted a fighting stance.

'Assuming the double negative was unintentional,' Milton said, 'I beg to differ.' He picked up a bundle of papers from a side table. Clara could see that they were covered with writing and sketches. 'You have no idea what these notes are worth. Some of the ideas in here could change the nature of warfare in the modern age. Projects I am really looking forward to pursuing, once I've left this rather dreary world and its rather dreary people behind. Present company included. Now, if you'll excuse me.'

As he spoke, two figures rose from the two

armchairs between Milton and the others. The high
backs of the chairs had concealed their presence until
now. One of the figures was Silhouette. Clara was
surprised to see that the other was a young man she
recognised.

'Oswald?'

'Oh dear,' Oswald said. 'I think this could be a bit
embarrassing. You see, I'm not really Oswald.'

'What?'

Clara watched in shocked surprise as the young
man's features blurred and changed. His face became
rounder, his dark hair was suddenly an unruly mass
of fair hair.

'Any more than I am Jim,' the figure said. The face
changed again, collapsing in on itself, then expanding
again into a different shape – a reptilian face similar to
Vastra's. 'Or Festin.'

Then, abruptly, the man had no face at all. Just a
blank visage punctuated only by the most basic
shapes of eyes, nose, mouth. 'I am everyone and no
one. I am Affinity.'

'Yeah,' Jenny said, 'well some of us have seen your
tricks before and whoever you are, you ain't stopping
us.'

'Not quite right, I'm afraid,' Milton said. 'It's you
that isn't stopping me.'

He strode purposefully towards them. Affinity and
Silhouette stepped aside deferentially to let him pass.

Vastra, Jenny and Clara closed together, barring the man's way. As Milton approached them, Silhouette opened her arms, fingers extended.

Something hit Clara hard on the back. She winced, turning instinctively to see who was behind her. But there was no one. Beside her, first Jenny then Vastra cried out in surprise and pain. From the corner of her eye, Clara saw movement. She turned – in time to see a book fly off the nearest bookcase. It flew across the room, covers beating the air like wings, heading straight for Clara. She batted it away. But the book didn't fall – it came back at her like an enraged bird.

More books followed, swirling round Clara, Jenny and Vastra. A maelstrom of paper beating at them incessantly. She saw Vastra grab a book out of the air, and rip it in two. It dropped to the floor, still for a moment, then the pages ripped themselves from the broken binding and flew up again in Vastra's face. Through the blizzard, Clara saw Milton hurrying out of the room. She tried to cry out, but her words were choked off by a another barrage of paper.

Jenny's hands were a blur, swiping at the attacking volumes, smashing them aside. In contrast it was all Clara could do to stay on her feet and keep the books and paper from her face.

'Stop her,' Vastra cried through the noise of beating paper. 'You have to stop her, Jenny.'

Somehow Jenny was making headway, forcing

her way through the blizzard of paper and cloth and leather towards where Silhouette stood watching. Finally she was close enough to reach the woman, hurling herself forwards and knocking Silhouette to the ground. But it made no difference, more books flew from the shelves to strike at Jenny.

'Necklace!' Clara yelled. 'Get her necklace.'

She had no idea if it would help, but it was all she could think of. She caught snatches of what was happening through the flurry of pages. Glimpses, like juddering frames from an old film. Jenny reaching for the crystal round Silhouette's neck. Grabbing it. Snapping it free. Hurling it away across the room.

Nothing changed. The books kept coming. The crystal clattered to the wooden floor not far from Clara, gleaming as it caught the light. With a supreme effort, Clara shoved through the books, turning her back into them as if forcing her way through a gale. Three steps, that was all – surely she could manage just three steps. It seemed to take for ever then she was staring down at the crystal, seeing multiple images of her face reflected in crimson, staring back at her.

She stamped down hard with the heel of her boot.

The crystal shattered, blood ray shards spraying out across the floor.

At once the noise and confusion stopped. Books fell to the floor. Slowly Jenny got to her feet.

Silhouette struggled up after her, staring round at

the debris strewn across the floor. 'What have I done?' she said, her voice little more than a whisper.

'Not enough,' the blank-faced man said, and hurled himself at her.

In a flash of movement, Jenny was between them, grappling with Affinity. The man's hand reached up for Jenny's neck. A glint of red as it moved. Vastra and Clara both rushed to help. Clara grabbed the man's hand, dragging it back, wrenching the ring from his finger and dropping it to the floor. Again, she stamped down.

And again the effect was immediate. Affinity seemed to sag, stepping away from Jenny. His face slowly filled out, assuming the aspect of the showman at the Carnival who had introduced Vastra to the audience as the Lizard Woman. Then, in rapid succession, he was Festin again, then Jim, and finally Oswald. He looked round, startled and confused as his features slowly faded away again to a blank.

'My head,' he said slowly. 'I can… *think*.'

'We are free of him,' Silhouette said. She enfolded Affinity in an embrace. After a moment she stepped away again. 'Thank you,' she said to Clara, Vastra and Jenny.

'Don't thank us just yet,' Clara said. 'We still have to stop Milton.'

'He has gone to his vessel,' Silhouette said. 'This way.'

But before she could move, there was a sound from the other side of the room – a sudden hiss of escaping gas. The dark cloud inside the glass sphere was churning and swirling. As they watched, it thinned, the sphere slowly becoming transparent, empty.

'We're too late,' Clara realised. 'He's released the cloud.'

'How do we stop it?' Vastra demanded.

Silhouette and Affinity looked at each other. 'I don't think we can,' Affinity said.

'Milton may know a way,' Silhouette suggested.

'Then show us where he is,' Jenny said.

The entrance to the underground chamber where Milton's ship was hidden was under the main staircase. A simple wooden door looked as though it should lead into a store cupboard.

'There are steps down,' Affinity explained.

But when they opened the door, they were confronted by a metal shutter. There was no way to open it.

Clara hammered her fist against the metal in frustration. 'He's sealed it. How do we open this?'

Neither Silhouette nor Affinity had any idea. 'He controls everything from his study,' Silhouette offered.

'That computer screen,' Clara said. 'It's worth a try.'

*

A dark cloud poured out like smoke from the chimney of the house. It spread thinner and thinner across the sky, wafting its way over London, slowly sinking down through the air.

Several streets away, a dog started to bark angrily. Close by, a jostled pedestrian decided that after all he did mind. A shopkeeper's frustration with an indecisive customer started to boil over.

A palpable tension was building in the air. Expressions changed as smiles became frowns, as people's good will and tolerance ebbed away without them even realising what had changed. The mildest of people took offence, the most affable snarled in rage. Arguments became shouting matches, which became fights, which became bloody.

Slowly at first, spreading from Milton's house, people's emotions began to get the better of them. Anger clouded judgement.

Silhouette and Affinity stood slightly apart from the others as Vastra worked at the screen.

'So many deaths,' Silhouette said quietly, sadly. 'So much suffering.'

Affinity's face remained a blank. But his voice now had some texture, echoing the sadness and regret. 'It was not our doing.'

'We should have fought him.'

'We did. We tried. Remember?'

Silhouette nodded. 'I remember. I remember everything.'

At the screen, Vastra gave an exasperated sigh. 'It's useless. The data is all gone. He must have erased it remotely.'

As she spoke, the screen flickered and an image appeared. Milton stared back at them from the tablet. Behind him they could see the cramped interior of his ship's flight deck.

'You really cannot be so naive as to think I would leave you any way to stop me, can you?' His voice emerged clearly from the device. 'I'd say come and join me, but as you can see I'm a little short of space. Just as you are all a little short of time.'

'You won't get away with this,' Clara said.

'Another melodramatic stock phrase you've always wanted to use?' Milton said. 'Sadly, as inaccurate as the first. And is that Silhouette and Affinity I can see behind you?' He gave a little wave. 'I'm so sorry that you'll also be affected by the cloud. Very soon, I expect. You are in the eye of the storm, as it were, so you might have a little more time before it permeates the whole of London's atmosphere.'

Silhouette stepped closer to the screen. 'You have made us do terrible things,' she said.

Milton smiled sympathetically. 'I made you into a weapon, my dear. Weapons do terrible things. That is rather the point of them.'

'It is a mistake to turn your own weapons against yourself.'

'I think I'm quite safe down here, thank you. Oh, but there is one thing you could still do for me.' He leaned forward slightly. 'Leave the screen on. I would like to see you all when the anger cloud does reach you. I'd like to watch you kill each other in rage and fury.'

'The Doctor will stop it,' Clara said. She tried to sound as if she believed it. Judging by Milton's amused reaction, she didn't succeed.

'I am monitoring the deployment of the cloud quite closely,' he said. 'So if that should happen, which I very much doubt, I'll know all about it. Good luck to him, I say. Although, of course, I don't really mean that.'

'Turn it off,' Clara said.

Vastra wiped her hand across the screen and it faded to black. The sound of Milton's laughter lingered just a moment longer then it too was gone.

'That man makes me so angry,' Jenny said, her hands bunched into tight fists.

'Let us hope that is the only thing making you angry,' Vastra said. 'How long do we have?'

'Not long,' Affinity said.

'Then let's get thinking,' Clara told them. 'We have to leave the cloud to the Doctor and hope he can deal with it. We need to sort out Milton.'

'And how do we do that?' Jenny asked.

'Like Silhouette said, we have weapons.' Clara nodded at Silhouette and Affinity. 'Let's work out how to use them.'

Chapter

19

Told off for misbehaving, little Betty Naismith didn't lower her head and mutter an apology as usual. Instead she slapped her nursemaid hard across the face.

In the pub on the corner of the same street, a quiet regular customer yelled uncontrollably at the barmaid that 'I'll be with you in a minute' wasn't good enough.

Not far away, a boy's 'excuse me' as he inadvertently knocking into an old woman was answered with a crack of her walking stick across his back.

All across the city, tempers simmered close to boiling point, ready to explode at any moment.

But as the rest of London slowly began its dissolution into anger, hatred and imminent violence, there was one small area that resisted. Watching the emotional indicator levels overlaid on a map of the city, Milton frowned. That made no sense. How come the cloud was having less effect in that one particular area?

He zoomed the map on his screen to a higher level of detail. Things became both clearer and more vexing.

'The Doctor?' he wondered out loud. But what could the Doctor be doing at the Carnival of Curiosities that would hold back the effects of the cloud?

At the increased magnitude, he saw that another marker had shown up on the map – closing on the area that was resisting the effects. Milton's frown became a smile and he nodded with satisfaction. Whatever the Doctor was doing – and he was quite sure it must be the Doctor – it would soon stop. Empath had found him.

A darkness was permeating the thin layer of smog that lay over London like a grubby reflection of the snow-covered ground. The Doctor could see it swirling and thickening above them as the show got under way.

A handful of coins had persuaded the lad on the gate to open the Carnival of Curiosities for free. A folded banknote added further encouragement for him to yell at the top of his voice that there was no admittance charge and that the show of a lifetime was about to start.

Inquisitive and intrigued, the crowds gathered round the open area where the Strong Man and the jugglers usually performed. They were not to be disappointed. In fact, the Doctor reflected, they had to be positively enthralled, enraptured, and lots of other positive things beginning with 'en'.

He was off to a good start. Some impressive juggling was followed by a jaw-dropping display of acrobatics. The Doctor had not been specific but he had made it very clear to each and every one of the performers that they were to give the show of their lives. Or else, their lives might very soon end. The Doctor didn't see himself as a natural performer, not in this incarnation, but he managed to rouse the crowd, building the level of anticipation.

The audience was growing bigger by the moment as more and more people heard the cries of delight and whoops of excitement. Strax was a big hit. No one was quite sure what to make of him – was he a genuine Strong Man, or a clown? When he threatened to obliterate anyone who laughed as he attempted to juggle with cannon balls, the crowd burst into a spontaneous mixture of applause and hysterics.

And all the time, the cloud above them gathered and darkened, as if focused on this small area of amusement and goodwill in a city now wallowing in confusion and anger. Timing was everything, the Doctor reflected, as the crowd laughed and clapped again. He could just make out the distinctive shape of Empath pushing his way slowly through. The Doctor glanced up again. Was it his imagination, or did the cloud now look like a giant claw waiting to strike down at him?

He nodded to Strax. 'Keep it going,' he mouthed. Then the Doctor walked over to the edge of the assembled crowd, to the point where Empath was emerging.

The marker that represented Empath was now right at the heart of the area resisting the cloud's effects. It wouldn't be long now, Milton thought. Empath would deal with the Doctor and then the cloud would do its worst. Checking other areas, he was pleased to see that fights were breaking out in several pubs. Police sent to calm the trouble were joining in. Another hour or two and the entire city would be in chaos.

A chime from the communications systems surprised him. It was probably the Doctor's friends, ready to beg for their lives. Yes, he decided, he would make the connection. He enjoyed seeing people beg, especially when he knew it was a completely futile act.

Sure enough, the familiar face of the Doctor's young friend Clara appeared on the screen. Milton could see the lizard woman and her maid behind. There was no sign of Silhouette or Affinity, but they were probably there somewhere. Unless they had already succumbed and killed each other, that was a pleasant thought.

'Please,' Clara said, 'you have to stop this. It's getting out of hand.'

'That is sort of the point, actually,' Milton told her. 'Was there anything else?'

'But people are *dying*. Don't you care about that at all?'

'Not really, I'm afraid.' Milton leaned back in his command chair. 'I assume you've been trying to find a way to open the security door and get down here. I did see that it registered an attack with a blunt instrument as well as a crude attempt to hack the locking software.'

'You can't blame us for trying, can you?' the maid Jenny told him.

'Oh not at all. I applaud the effort.' He clapped his hands together a couple of times to make the point. 'But there really isn't any way to get to me or to stop the cloud. So…'

He paused. That was odd. There was another message coming in.

'I'm so sorry,' Milton said, 'I'm going to have to put you on hold just for a minute. Have a nice day.'

He switched channels. His first thought was that it was the secondary comms link from the library, but the face that appeared on the screen now was as surprising as it was unexpected. Milton felt suddenly cold. They'd found him – how could they have found him?

'You know who I am?' the pale face on the screen asked.

'Of course, Senior Deputy Shadow Architect.' Milton struggled to keep the nerves out of his voice. 'I must apologise for the abrupt end to our last conversation, but as you will recall I rather fancied escaping before you could have me summarily executed on the spot.'

The Senior Deputy smiled. 'A lucky escape for both of us, perhaps. You see, we have been watching your progress very carefully.'

'You know where I am?'

'Oh, please. We've known for weeks.'

'Then why haven't you—'

'Arrested you? *Executed* you? Because your work intrigued us. This latest experiment, the cloud now dissipating over the city of London, is especially interesting.'

Milton was surprised. 'Interesting? To the Shadow Proclamation?'

'Assuming the cloud could be used to dispense any emotion in concentrated form it might provide a useful way of, what shall we say? Of calming populations in times of crisis. Ensuring that cool heads prevail. Of course, I appreciate you are demonstrating the exact opposite here, but I would assume the principle holds good?'

'Er, yes,' Milton said quickly. 'Yes, of course. I'm sorry,' he went on, 'but am I to take it that the Shadow Proclamation is interested in coming to some sort of understanding? You did sentence me to death, as I recall.'

The Senior Deputy Shadow Architect waved a hand. 'Oh, please. A misunderstanding. Forget all about it. The sentence has been rescinded. Or at least, postponed.'

'Postponed, I see. And what do I need to do to ensure it is lifted permanently? I hope you don't want me to stop the cloud from consuming London, because I have to admit that I can't. It's too late for that.'

The Senior Deputy nodded. 'We suspected that was the case. Clearly there are some enhancements that can still be made to the weapon.'

'It is a project that is very much under development,' Milton agreed.

'Then our proposition is simple. Come and work for us, finish the development of this and perhaps other weapons under the auspices of the Shadow Proclamation and you will also be assured our protection. Along with a full pardon for any past misdemeanours.'

'Including any you don't already know about?' Milton asked.

'Are there any we don't already know about?'

'Modesty forbids.' Milton smiled. This was turning out better than he had ever expected. Perhaps under that righteous façade, the Shadow Proclamation was rather more draconian than people thought.

He turned to retrieve his pile of notes from a nearby control console. 'I do already have a few ideas that might be of interest in the areas of population control and the upholding of justice. If we can call it that.'

The Senior Deputy Shadow Architect smiled back as he saw Milton brandishing the sheaf of papers. 'I see that you understand exactly what is required.'

The further into the mass of people Empath went, the more their emotions pressed in upon him. By the time he emerged, to see the Doctor standing in front of him, he was confused and disoriented. The Doctor – he had been looking for the Doctor, and now here he was. But why? There was a vague sense that he should be angry with the Doctor. But the anger that had been welling up inside Empath and ready to burst out was now buried deep beneath the feelings he had absorbed as he pushed through the crowd.

The Doctor grabbed Empath by the hand and pulled him into the performance area. He hardly noticed as the Doctor slipped the ring from his middle finger. Didn't see the way the red crystal first cracked and then shattered as the Doctor touched it with the glowing end of his sonic screwdriver. All around him, people were laughing, clapping, enjoying themselves. Jugglers, acrobats, clowns, the Strong Man, everyone was brimming over with good humour.

'Do you feel it?' the Doctor said, shouting to be

heard above the appreciative roar of the crowd.

Behind him a fire-eater blew flames out of his mouth, toasting a marshmallow held out on a sword by his assistant who then offered it to a small boy standing nearby.

'Can you feel the emotion, the excitement, the well-being? Can you feel the love tonight?' The Doctor frowned. 'No, hang on, that's not right. Well, maybe it is.'

Empath was grinning as it flowed into him, looking round in childlike amazement and glee. 'It *is* wonderful,' he admitted.

'A happy undertaker.' The Doctor laughed. 'Not something you see every day.'

The sky was getting darker. A shadow passing over the Carnival. Empath looked up to see a huge dark pall of what looked like smoke. It seemed to gather itself above them.

'What's that?' he said, pointing upwards. Lots of people were pointing at the cloud now as it slowly drifted lower.

'Ah, well,' the Doctor said. 'That's something I need your help with. Take a deep breath.'

'What?'

'A deep breath, go on. Not real breath, of course. But draw in as much of that good feeling as you can. All the laughter and the mirth and the happiness. The confidence and appreciation and delight. Exhilaration and joy and elation. This is your world, after all – don't you remember? Don't you remember who you used to be? Who you *are*. Go on. Do it now.'

The cloud dipped lower. Empath breathed in the atmosphere around him. He could feel himself filling with emotion, overflowing with happiness. He was David Rutherford. He belonged here, along with the performers, along with his friends, bringing people joy and happiness...

Then, suddenly, it was dark. The cloud rushed towards the Doctor, towards Empath standing beside him, spilling over them like a waterfall. Cold and damp and unpleasant, deadening every thought. Somewhere, muffled by the heavy air, someone screamed.

'Now,' the Doctor said close to Empath's ear. 'Let it out. Just like you let the anger out into Milton's sphere. Let all the emotion of the crowd out now. Do it!'

Empath let it out. A great breath of emotion. The muffled screams had become cheers as the crowd watched what they thought was the latest act. He could hear the Doctor's voice, though he could not make out the words. But it felt good, it felt like the Doctor was encouraging and praising him as the darkness faded and cleared.

The effect rippled out across the sky. A wave running through the dark smog of anger and despair, washing it clean. The cloud faded, thinned, dissipated – its anger and rage cancelled out by the concentrated force of the joy and elation from the crowd.

The people applauded as they watched the air clear. For the first time in a while, the sun shone down through a hole in the fog, illuminating the Carnival of Curiosities like a spotlight shining down at a huge circus ring filled with performers and watched by the laughing audience.

'Well done,' the Doctor said, and he was laughing as well. 'Really – *really* well done.'

Empath – David – was laughing too. He took a bow, sweeping off his hat. The Doctor caught hold of the long, black silk that trailed from it, unwinding the material and pulling it away. So that when David replaced the top hat on his head it was no longer swathed in black.

Transformed from undertaker, the Ringmaster raised his hands above his head for calm and quiet. They waited expectantly.

'And for our next trick…' he began.

Chapter
20

They had moved from Milton's study to the library. Clara and Jenny stood at the window, the curtains drawn back and the shutters open. Vastra was talking quietly to Affinity and Silhouette, who had activated a small viewing screen close to the now empty glass sphere.

'I think it's clearing,' Clara said, staring up at the sky. 'It's not as dark as it was.'

Vastra was working at the screen. 'You are right. Milton has this calibrated to track the progress of the cloud. It has dissipated.'

'So the Doctor's done it,' Jenny said, elated. 'Well,' she added more calmly, 'no surprise there.'

'Which just leaves us Milton to deal with.' Vastra said. 'I rerouted the communications feed to the study terminal here, so I expect we'll hear from him soon.'

'Let's see him put a positive spin on this, then,' Clara said.

Milton did indeed seem in a good mood when his

face appeared on the screen a few moments later. Or at least, he was not too downhearted.

'My congratulations,' he announced. 'It seems I did indeed underestimate the Doctor.'

'You are not the first to make that mistake,' Vastra told him.

'I doubt I shall be the last either. But we must all learn from our mistakes. So when I've analysed the observation data I can set about eliminating whatever weakness the Doctor found in my weapon.'

'Really?' Clara said. 'You're trapped down there. You don't really think you can just carry on like this never happened do you?'

'What would you suggest, my dear?'

'Well for starters,' Clara said, 'I'd suggest you don't call me "my dear" if you value your kneecaps. Then it seems to me that surrender is your best option.'

'Surrender?' Milton seemed to consider this. 'No, sorry. Not an option I like at all, actually. And if I may say so, I think perhaps you are overestimating the extent of your little victory.'

'We've got you trapped like a rat in your own basement,' Jenny said. 'Your so-called weapons are all gone. So you tell us what exactly we've overestimated.'

'If you stay down there, you will eventually starve,' Vastra added. 'If you leave in your ship, the Shadow Proclamation will immediately spot the engine signature. I imagine they have forces in the area as they must have tracked you to this system or you'd have left a long time ago. So surrender to us and let the Doctor plead your case.'

'Plead my case?' Milton echoed. 'Oh, you mean argue for some sort of reduced sentence so that instead of being executed I just get locked up for ever. Mmmm.' He stroked his beard thoughtfully. 'No, doesn't sound that great, actually. Especially as I've had a better offer. So if you'll excuse me, I'll just be on my way.'

'A better offer?' Vastra said. 'What offer would that be?'

'Someone else wants your horrible weapons?' Clara asked.

'Oh I'm sorry, I should have mentioned it earlier. But well, one doesn't like to boast. The Senior Deputy Shadow Architect has just been in touch. Offering complete immunity. A pardon. In fact, the Shadow Proclamation would rather like me to go and develop my horrible weapons for them.'

'The Doctor always offers last chances,' Clara said. 'So this is yours. Just give up the weapons. Come out of your bunker down there and we can help you find some other way to make a fortune or whatever it is you want to do.'

'Not very tempted, I'm afraid. So if it's all right with you, I'll just say my goodbyes and be on my way. Oh, and it actually is "goodbye", I'm afraid. You see, I really can't let any of you live after this. I suppose it's to do with pride.'

'What do you mean?' Vastra demanded.

'Well, pride and also of course I do so hate anyone to get the better of me,' Milton went on, as if she hadn't spoken. 'So I'm afraid the Doctor and all of you really have to go. Once I'm well clear I shall be launching distronic missiles to destroy this whole area.'

'You're going to destroy London?' Clara said, appalled.

'Well, most of southern Britain, really. Sorry about that. Anyway, I'd better be going. And I imagine you have some goodbyes of your own to say to each other. I wish I could say it's been a pleasure.'

The screen went black.

The pre-flight checks were complete. While the computer went through the final activation sequence, Milton leafed through his notes. Yes, there were some ideas in here that would certainly interest the Shadow Proclamation. He gathered the notes together and rested them on the console in front of him as the ship slowly turned on its axis and started along the gentle slope that led up to the launch ramp.

The ramp was concealed inside the coach house. The horses in the stables beside it would get a shock, though the blast shielding would make sure they were unharmed. At least until he launched his missiles. It was a shame, Milton thought, as he had quite enjoyed his enforced stay here. That said, the city was a mess – maybe levelling it, together with much of the surrounding countryside, would allow the primitive natives to rebuild something rather better in its place. He was probably doing them a favour, in the long run.

He checked his safety harness was securely fastened as the ship tilted backwards. A few moments later there was a burst of thrust from behind. Milton was slammed back into his seat as the ship shot up the ramp. His papers slipped from the console, falling to the floor.

The wooden doors shattered into splintered fragments as the ship exploded out of the coach house. Smoke and flame trailing behind it, the small craft climbed rapidly through the smoggy air before bursting through the clouds and into open sky.

Clara watched from the window.

'There he goes,' she said.

'Don't feel bad about what's going to happen,' Silhouette told her, resting a hand gently on Clara's shoulder. 'He had a choice. For all his charm, he is a sadistic murderer.'

'Will he launch the missiles?' Jenny asked.

'He won't have time,' Vastra told her.

'We hope,' Clara murmured.

*

The G-force eased off as the ship reached the upper atmosphere. Milton quickly checked the instruments.

'All systems are online and functioning normally,' the computer reported in a husky female voice. Milton had selected it from an option palette of over a hundred possible voices.

'Alone at last,' he said. 'Just you and me.'

'And the Dekseller-class Smart Torpedoes approaching rapidly from sector nine,' the computer reported.

'What? Show me!' Milton stared at the main screen, his brow furrowed with worry and disbelief as he watched two tiny points of light approaching the marker that represented his own ship.

'Analysis confirms that the torpedoes are standard smart weapons as deployed by the Shadow Proclamation. Impact in 57 seconds. Evasive action advised.'

Milton switched to manual control. The computer was predictable, and the torpedoes would be programmed to expect the standard responses, evasion techniques and countermeasures. '

'Seems someone at the Shadow Proclamation didn't get the message,' he said as he swung the ship in a wide arc. 'Open a communications channel to the Senior Deputy Shadow Architect. Call him back at the communications node he contacted me from before.'

A small screen showed the countdown to impact. Milton kept an eye on it as the communication system connected. For the moment, the number was remaining at about the 50-second mark as he dodged the ship round. If he could keep away from them for long enough the torpedoes should run out of fuel before he did. But it would take a long time and a lot of concentration.

'Connection established.'

The main screen flickered and the image of the Senior Deputy Shadow Architect appeared. He smiled pleasantly. 'And what can I do for you, Orestes?'

'You can get these torpedoes off my tail,' Milton said, struggling to steer the ship wide of the approaching weapons.

The smile became sympathetic. 'Ah, I'm afraid I can't help you there.'

'If you give me the command access code, I can disable them myself,' Milton told him. 'There's a standard protocol, you must know it.'

The ship juddered as one of the torpedoes narrowly missed. It shot past, already swinging round to come back at the ship.

'I'm sorry, I don't know the code you mean.'

'You must!'

'In fact, I confess I don't really have any idea what you're talking about.'

'What?' Milton was finding it hard to concentrate on

avoiding the torpedoes and follow what the Deputy said. 'It's a standard code.' He had to shout above the warning klaxon now sounding in the cabin. 'It's given to all senior officials of the Shadow Proclamation – you *must* know it.'

'Ah, now I think that might be the problem.' The sympathetic smile was back as the man nodded slowly. 'Who exactly do you think I am?'

Milton dropped the ship suddenly and one of the torpedoes shot past just above him. 'You're the Senior Deputy Shadow Architect,' he said through gritted teeth. But even as he said it a terrible suspicion began to form in the back of his mind. 'Unless...' He stared at the screen in disbelief.

The screen where the pale, drawn features of the Senior Deputy blurred and shimmered before settling into a blank face, devoid of features or expression.

'Affinity?'

'I'm flattered that you even remember me,' Affinity said. 'But really, you should have realised sooner. Did you actually think anyone would offer *you* a pardon?'

'I saw who I wanted – saw what I needed to see,' Milton realised. 'Heard what I wanted to hear.'

Somehow, even though it was a blank, the face on the screen seemed to be smiling back at him. 'I believe that is called "working as designed".'

Milton tore his attention away from the screen, just in time to dodge one of the torpedoes. He had to maintain concentration. He could get through this. He forced himself to smile back at Affinity.

'You'll forgive me, but I am rather busy right now. Rest assured, though, that as soon as I have dealt with these torpedoes I shall launch my own missiles at you. Now, if you will excuse me, I need to concentrate, so if you've quite finished gloating.'

He reached out to cut the communications link.

'I wasn't gloating,' Affinity said quietly. 'I just wanted to keep you talking. I just wanted to keep the link open between us here and your ship.' The screen cut out. Affinity's voice faded. The last that Milton heard was: 'Silhouette says goodbye.'

Then he was alone again, accelerating past one torpedo and dipping under the other. He could do this. They were getting closer. He looked at the countdown.

Time to Impact: 23

He'd allowed himself to be distracted. Concentrate, and he could do this.

'I just wanted to keep the link open…' What had Affinity meant by that?

Never mind. Something to consider later. Concentrate.

'Silhouette says goodbye.'

Concentrate.

Silhouette? Oh no. Please, no.

Milton risked looking down, towards where his notes and papers had fallen. There was just one sheet of paper lying close to the command chair – where were the others? He swung the ship sideways.

Time to Impact: **17**

He dared to look down again. The paper rippled, as if stirred by a breeze. His handwriting dissolved as he watched, smudging and spreading. The ink seemed to be moving, flowing, coming together to form a single word across the page.

Time to Impact: **13**

He leaned down, staring closer. The word swam into focus:

Sorry

Concentrate. Ignore it.

Time to Impact: **10**

The two torpedoes were closing from different sides. This was it – this was his chance. Time it exactly, accelerate away at just the right moment, and the two torpedoes would miss his ship and crash into each other. Problem solved.

Time to Impact: 7

At 3, Milton calculated. He reached for the main thruster boost control.

Time to Impact: 4

And a blizzard of paper shot across the cabin. A swarm of small folded birds, wings flapping in his face, edges cutting into him, stinging his eyes. The whole world was a swirl of white. Something cut sharply across his hand and he snatched it back with a yelp. He battered at the creatures with both hands, shouting and screaming in anger. A bird fluttered in front of his face, and he recognised the paper – recognised fragments of his own handwritten notes across its wings and body. He swatted it away angrily. Somehow he managed to clear the space in front of his eyes, just for a second.

Just long enough to see the screen.

Time to Impact: 1

Then the world exploded into light and fire.
A mass of flame burned impossibly in space for a

moment, consuming the oxygen that spilled from the exploding ship. Then the fireball collapsed in on itself. The shattered debris and fragmented remains of the ship spun silently away into the blackness.

And in the middle of it all, a single paper bird flapped its wings needlessly as it drifted into the distance, swallowed up by the perpetual night.

Chapter

21

The air above the Carnival of Curiosities was clear and bright where the cloud had dissipated. The London smog had not yet reclaimed the evening sky. High above Ringmaster Empath's outstretched hand, the heavens exploded in a sudden display of colour. Red, yellow, and orange blossomed out above the assembled crowd.

There were whoops and cheers, applause and gasps of awe. The air seemed to glow and shimmer, light dancing across before folding in on itself and fading to nothing…

The applause continued long after the lightshow had ended.

'I think the Shadow Proclamation has finally caught up with our friend Mr Milton,' the Doctor told Strax. 'I saw his ship launch earlier.'

'A clipper-class scoutship,' Strax said. 'Agile, but with little protective armament and woefully inadequate countermeasures.'

'Quod erat demonstrandum,' the Doctor agreed.

Strax frowned. 'Not a system I am familiar with.' He gestured at the sky, where the lights had now faded away and the smog was slowly rolling in to fill the space. 'The energy-discharge pattern of a Dekseller-class Smart Torpedo is highly distinctive.'

The Doctor suppressed a smile. 'The trouble with you, Strax, is that you take all the beauty out of life.'

'War is beautiful, Doctor.'

'Ah now, there I think we shall have to differ.'

They stood in silence for a few moments, watching the acrobats performing and Empath – or David as he now was again – enthusing the crowd and leading the applause.

'You must admit,' the Doctor said at last, 'that humans do have some talent and potential.' There was no answer. 'Mustn't you?'

Strax grunted. 'I have recently discovered a product of human ingenuity and engineering which I found quite impressive,' he said. 'Right here at this very entertainment hub.'

'Really?' the Doctor raised an eyebrow. 'Care to elaborate?'

'Gladly. The item may be obtained from one of these vending concessions.' He led the Doctor back through the crowd towards the Frost Fair. 'I believe it is called a toffee apple.'

*

'Unfortunately,' the Doctor explained to Clara, 'Strax didn't know you eat them. He thought they were for throwing at people.'

They had all spent the evening at Paternoster Row, Affinity and Silhouette included. But now the Doctor was itching to get back to the TARDIS. Clara knew it would do no good to suggest they spend a few days relaxing in Victorian London. She knew that look. But she did insist they say a proper goodbye rather than simply slipping away as the Doctor wanted.

Vastra, Jenny and Strax walked with them to where the TARDIS stood, thinly coated with snow. An icicle descended from the door handle and the windows were frosted over. Silhouette and Affinity were also there. Affinity wore his hat pulled down low so that the brim shadowed his empty face.

'I'd like to say it's been fun,' the Doctor said. Clara nudged him with her elbow. 'But, well, yes,' he admitted. 'It's had its moments.'

'Where you off to now, then?' Jenny asked.

'Who knows?' Clara said.

'No doubt there are enemies waiting to be vanquished,' Strax said. He slammed his fist into his open palm. 'Show them no mercy. Press home your initial assault with determination and brutality.'

'Thanks,' Clara told him, 'we'll do that.'

'We'll rain down toffee apples on them,' the Doctor promised, suppressing a smile.

'We shall see you again soon,' Vastra said, shaking the Doctor's hand. 'You know you are always welcome.'

'Thank you.'

'As are you,' Vastra said to Silhouette and Affinity.

'Will you be all right?' Clara asked them.

'They'll be fine,' the Doctor said before either of them could answer. 'Don't fuss. Come on.' He turned to unlock the TARDIS.

'We shall,' Silhouette agreed. She linked her arm through Affinity's.

'I don't know where we will go or what we will do, but Silhouette is right,' Affinity agreed.

'Won't you go back to the Carnival?' Clara asked.

'Perhaps,' Silhouette agreed. 'Or perhaps we shall set up on our own. The future is such an adventure, don't you think?'

'Oh, well said,' the Doctor told her, turning to bundle Clara into the TARDIS ahead of him. 'Well said indeed. Now come on, can't stand here gassing and dawdling all day, can we? No, we can't. Bye, then.'

As the distinctive sound of TARDIS engines faded away, the snow and ice and frost that had clung to its police box shell fell to the ground. An empty square on the pavement was all to show it had ever been there.

'Will you join us?' Vastra asked.

Silhouette shook her head. 'Perhaps another day.

But for now, we must make our own way, decide who we are and what we will do.'

'Thank you,' Affinity said. 'For everything.'

Two figures walked arm in arm along the Embankment. The woman wore a long scarlet cloak, the hood pulled up over her head. The man was dressed in a suit, his hat pulled down low.

They stopped above the Frost Fair, looking out across the frozen Thames. The light played across their faces – one delicate and beautiful, the other empty and blank.

Then the blank face seemed to shimmer. It dissolved into various other faces, flickering through them as the man spoke.

'Who would you like me to be?' he asked.

The woman reached up, her fingers gently stroking his cheek. 'I love you for who you are, not what you look like,' she said. 'Just be yourself.'

And his features settled finally into the smile of a young man in love.

Acknowledgements

A novel is always a collaborative process, a *Doctor Who* novel even more so.

Thanks are therefore due not only to Steve Tribe for sterling editorial advice, and to Lizzy Gaisford and Albert DePetrillo for being BBC Books, but also to everyone involved with bringing the Doctor to our screens and pages – especially in his most recent incarnation.

I hope we've done him justice!

BBC

DOCTOR WHO

The Crawling Terror

MIKE TUCKER

ISBN 978-0-8041-4090-4

'Well, I doubt you'll ever see a bigger insect.'

Gabby Nichols is putting her son to bed when she hears her daughter cry out. 'Mummy, there's a daddy longlegs in my room!' Then the screaming starts… Kevin Alperton is on his way to school when he is attacked by a mosquito. A big one. Then things get dangerous.

But it isn't the dead man cocooned inside a huge mass of web that worries the Doctor. It isn't the swarming, mutated insects that make him nervous.

With the village cut off from the outside world, and the insects becoming more and more dangerous, the Doctor knows that unless he can decode the strange symbols engraved on an ancient stone circle, and unravel a mystery dating back to the Second World War, no one is safe.

An original novel featuring the Twelfth Doctor and Clara, as played by Peter Capaldi and Jenna Coleman

BBC
DOCTOR WHO
The Blood Cell

JAMES GOSS

ISBN 978-0-8041-4092-8

'Release the Doctor – or the killing will start.'

An asteroid in the furthest reaches of space – the most secure prison for the most dangerous of criminals. The Governor is responsible for the cruellest murderers. So he's not impressed by the arrival of the man they're calling the most dangerous criminal in the quadrant. Or, as he prefers to be known, the Doctor.

But when the new prisoner immediately sets about trying to escape, and keeps trying, the Governor sets out to find out why.

Who is the Doctor and what's he really doing here? And who is the young woman who comes every day to visit him, only to be turned away by the guards?

When the killing finally starts, the Governor begins to get his answers…

An original novel featuring the Twelfth Doctor and Clara, as played by Peter Capaldi and Jenna Coleman

BBC
DOCTOR WHO
Engines of War

GEORGE MANN

ISBN 978-0-553-44766-8

'The death of billions is as nothing to us Doctor,
if it helps defeat the Daleks.'

The Great Time War has raged for centuries, ravaging the
universe. Scores of human colony planets are now overrun by
Dalek occupation forces. A weary, angry Doctor leads a flotilla
of Battle TARDISes against the Dalek stronghold but in the
midst of the carnage, the Doctor's TARDIS crashes to a planet
below: Moldox.

As the Doctor is trapped in an apocalyptic landscape,
Dalek patrols roam amongst the wreckage, rounding up the
remaining civilians. But why haven't the Daleks simply killed
the humans?

Searching for answers the Doctor meets Cinder, a young Dalek
hunter. Their struggles to discover the Dalek plan take them
from the ruins of Moldox to the halls of Gallifrey, and set in
motion a chain of events that will change everything. And
everyone.

An epic novel of the Great Time War
featuring the War Doctor, as played by John Hurt